SHE SHIVERED
WITH DELIGHT

as his hands moved slowly along her back, drawing her closer and closer until their bodies seemed to mold into one. His lips came down to meet hers in a gentle kiss that lingered and hardened until her lips surrendered and parted under his demand. Then there was no time for thinking, no time for anything but each other. . . .

DARE
TO
LOVE

by

Glenna Finley

A SIGNET BOOK

NEW AMERICAN LIBRARY

TIMES MIRROR

Copyright © 1977 by Glenna Finley

SIGNET TRADEMARK REG. U.S. PAT. OFF. AND FOREIGN COUNTRIES
REGISTERED TRADEMARK—MARCA REGISTRADA
HECHO EN CHICAGO, U.S.A.

SIGNET, SIGNET CLASSICS, MENTOR, PLUME AND MERIDIAN BOOKS
are published by The New American Library, Inc.,
1301 Avenue of the Americas, New York, New York 10019

FIRST SIGNET PRINTING, JUNE, 1977

1 2 3 4 5 6 7 8 9

PRINTED IN THE UNITED STATES OF AMERICA

For Donald and Duncan

He either fears his Fate too much,
   Or his deserts are small,
That dares not put it to the touch,
   To win or lose it all.

—MARQUIS OF MONTROSE

Chapter One

All the promising omens for the advent of spring were in evidence that May morning in Helsinki—Finland's capital city. Mannerheimintie, the main thoroughfare, was alive with people on their way to work; cars nudged each other for position at the traffic lights alongside the big Olympic-stadium complex, and farther down, pedestrians lined for streetcars near the impressive white Finlandia Hall. By contrast, the park on either side of the building had only the rare pedestrian and dog walker at that hour of the morning. Later in the day there would be a crowd of critics surrounding the outdoor chessboard with its waist-high pieces, while the younger set of Helsinki would play on the multiheaded dragon statue nearby, which was a simple fallen tree until an enterprising architect had added monster heads to several of the branches. Instantly it had been turned into a splendid beast waiting for St. George to come along in the guise of a small Finnish girl or boy.

That morning, however, the two adults standing by its lower head had other things on their minds

1

besides the slaying of dragons. One of the men watched an elderly lady walking her wirehaired dachshund past on the sidewalk and waited until the pair were safely out of hearing before he said irritably to his companion, "I don't know why I was fool enough to meet you here. You could have gotten your message across on the telephone without taking any risk."

"Since you've neglected to return my calls, our employer decided that you needed a more stringent reminder," the other snapped. "They want a definite date for delivery. Your promises are wearing thin, and so is our patience."

"I told Saari I was doing the best I could. Didn't he get the news to you?" When there was no immediate answer, the man's eyelids hooded his suspicious gaze. "You *did* get that last report I gave him, didn't you?"

"After a time. Saari unfortunately didn't like our terms and thought he could do better on his own."

"So?" There was no expression in the monosyllable.

"So we decided it would be easier without dealing with Saari. He'd outlived his usefulness." The other's grin was without humor, mirroring the wooden dragon's head by his elbow with its curling saturnine lips.

There was a pause. Then the younger man said in a low tone, "And there'll be no more contacts with Mr. Saari?"

"I shouldn't think so. Unless some fool fisherman gets an unexpected catch in his nets, which is highly unlikely. Now you know what you're dealing with," he went on casually. "We expect your delivery on time—otherwise the information will be virtually useless."

"I said I'd try. For God's sake, man—"

The other interrupted him. "You'd do well to ignore hope of divine intervention. Saari was still calling for it when he was being wired to a block of concrete. Afterward he didn't make any noise at all. You should remember." As footsteps sounded along the path, he shot a look toward the chessboard, where a young woman with brown hair had paused to survey the pieces. "We've talked enough. No more meetings until the delivery. Arrange that through the usual Danish channels." He turned and hurried down a path which angled away from the newcomer, his long strides covering the ground rapidly.

The other man left almost as abruptly, walking up the hill toward the Mannerheimintie and dodging across the street through the lanes of traffic. An instant later, he had disappeared around the corner.

The young woman who had quickened her steps to intercept them watched their disappearing backs with a rueful expression. "Damn!" she said feelingly to the nearest head on the dragon tree. "They needn't have run away as if I had the plague. Now I'll *have* to go back to the hotel and ask which streetcar I'm supposed to take." She took a minute to admire the handsome creation by her side and patted the wooden nose. "I don't suppose you understand English either," she confided, "and it doesn't do me any good to use a Finnish phrase book, because every word has eighty-seven different letters in it—mostly consonants which are completely unpronounceable." She shoved her hands in the pockets of her suede topcoat. "Oh, well, I can walk back and ask directions of the hotel porter—the exercise will be good for me." She gave the head a farewell pat. "Nice meeting you, chum. If you ever decide to go traveling, we could use you in Central Park."

It was a full half-hour later when Lynda Garrett got off a modern tram and watched it turn the corner out of sight. She took a deep breath, feeling as if her last link with anything familiar had just been severed. A glance at the street sign showed she was at the junction of Mannerheimintie and Lonnrotinkatu.

"Big deal," she murmured to herself. "As if that helped." For another moment she tried to pronounce the Swedish translation, Lonnrotsgatan, on the sign and then shook her head despairingly. She might as well have faced a Swahili phrase book or an Arabic crossword puzzle.

As she waited for a break in the traffic to cross the busy street, she decided it was a good thing that travel agents didn't tell prospective tourists to Finland the stark truth. That old saw about everybody speaking English might have some merit, but after her sign-language fiasco with the conductor of the streetcar, Lynda had dark suspicions about *that*, too.

She was thankful that her inward perturbation didn't show. The only glances that she seemed to be attracting from passersby were the masculine kind that didn't need translating anywhere in the world. Her lips curved in a wry smile. If she had to ask directions from a stranger, it had better be from a Scandinavian who didn't give her a sweeping ankle-to-chin glance that tabulated vital statistics en route. Evidently the Finnish men kept themselves occupied that way during their nine months of winter and the three months they spent waiting for summer to come.

Lynda's glance settled finally on a likely candidate, a tall, broad-shouldered man in his early thirties with a shock of fair hair, who was wearing the uniform of Scandinavian businessmen—a dark suit and immaculate white shirt. As she watched him approach, the brisk breeze prompted him to stop and shrug into the gabardine raincoat he carried over his arm.

Lynda didn't wait for a better opportunity. "I beg your pardon," she said, enunciating slowly and distinctly as she walked up to him. "Do you possibly speak English?"

His head jerked around in surprise. A pair of blue eyes as frosty as a Finnish lake in winter met hers and then did the usual appraisal of her figure. His frown deepened when his glance came back up and stopped. Evidently American women who accosted strangers on the streets weren't in his letter to Santa Claus . . . especially medium-sized, brown-haired ones with gray eyes. Lynda made a mental note to discard her pageboy hairstyle and change to a brighter lipstick over the weekend. It was strange that the other Finnish men she'd encountered since she left the hotel hadn't indicated any disapproval. She was still mulling that over when she said, "Never mind, forget the whole thing. I'd say 'sorry' in Finnish, but I don't know how," she added blithely, starting to turn away.

"Anteeksi," he replied in a deep tone that still showed suspicion.

"Anteeksi, then," Lynda said automatically before she whirled back. "You *do* speak English."

He looked down at her, slightly amused. "Tolerably well. What did you want to talk about?"

His words were so glib and unaccented that Lynda felt her spirits rise. "I want to get to the Arusha porcelain plant. The hotel porter told me to transfer to another streetcar or tram by the railroad station, but I've forgotten which one."

"Ummm." His response was noncommittal.

Lynda looked at him doubtfully. Maybe he was another one of those people like her breakfast waiter who professed to speak English and whose knowledge finally turned out to consist of "coffee," "tea," and "Your check, madam." Which hadn't helped when Lynda counted on grapefruit and a scrambled egg as well.

She went back to her careful enunciation. "You know of the Arusha plant?"

"I've heard of it." His stern expression softened.

"It's all right. You don't have to be so careful about using two-syllable words."

A wave of red swept along Lynda's cheekbones. "I just wanted to be sure," she said stiffly. "Actually you speak with hardly any accent," she added, trying for a gracious touch.

"You're very kind."

"Just truthful," she assured him, wondering if there was amusement in his tone or whether she "I have," he supplied when she paused expectantly.

"I have," he supplied when she paused expectantly.

"Very long?"

"Thirty years or so. I live on Long Island." As he saw her lips tighten with displeasure, he merely looked amused. "Your accent's pretty good, too."

"I'm sorry to have bothered you," Lynda said stiffly, wondering how she could have made such a fool mistake. The only American within blocks, and she had to accost him.

"Relax, Miss . . ." He checked her left hand for confirmation. "Miss . . . ?"

"Garrett. Lynda Garrett," she said, wondering why she didn't just turn and walk away.

Her voice must have revealed her feelings, because his look of amusement deepened as he said, "My name's Buchanan . . . Ross Buchanan. And you want a number-six streetcar marked direction Arusha. But I have a rental car around the corner, and I'm headed out that way myself." When she still hesitated, he added solemnly, "It's okay . . .

I'm single, solvent at the moment, and just mailed a postcard to my mother in Illinois. If you're worried about your virtue . . . I can produce references."

"I don't see what your references have to do with *my* virtue," she pointed out reasonably.

His eyes glinted in appreciation. "You have a point there."

"On the other hand, you look awfully respectable to be recruiting for anything dastardly," she said, noting the broad shoulders under their sober suiting. "Too respectable for a tourist. No camera . . . no sunglasses. That's why I was misled. Maybe I should check your passport, after all."

"Sorry, it's in the safe-deposit box at the hotel. I saw you at breakfast in the coffee shop there a little while ago."

"Then you must be telling the truth—I don't think a Finn has been in that hotel since it opened."

"Not at those prices," he agreed. "It's strictly for foreigners on expense accounts."

"I just hope that the accounting department will believe mine when I get home," she put in ruefully. "Is your car nearby?"

He nodded and gestured. "Up here in the middle of the block." As she fell into step beside him, he went on. "Is your trip to the porcelain plant for business or pleasure?"

Lynda dodged to let a young couple sauntering down the middle of the sidewalk pass by. "Business. I'm an assistant china buyer for a chain of

stores in New York." She named it proudly and
saw him nod.

"Your first trip?" he asked, drawing up beside a
blue Volvo at the curb and unlocking the car door.

"Yes. Why? Does it show?"

"Only around the edges. Actually, you look too
young for a job like that."

"I'm twenty-five." He made no comment, simply closed the door after he saw her settled in the
car and walked around to get behind the wheel.
Once he was seated, she went on, "I even took
French and Spanish lessons so I'd be ready when
my chance came for overseas buying trips. And
then what happened?"

"You were sent to Finland. . . ."

"Where you need a gypsy grandmother before
you can even read the street signs," she said somewhat bitterly as he waited for a break in the traffic
and then pulled out of the parking space. "And as
far as I'm concerned, the Swedish translation on
the bottom of the signs isn't any help."

He kept his attention fixed on the traffic, but
the laughter wrinkles at the edges of his eyes deepened. "You sound disillusioned."

"You'd be unhappy, too, if you'd pulled the
faux pas that I managed on the streetcar."

"Things couldn't have been too bad; you're still
in one piece."

"Yes, but the American image sagged again . . .
thanks to my idiocy." She shook her head, remem-
bering. "When I got on the blamed thing, I suddenly realized that I didn't know how much the

fare was, and absolutely nobody around me spoke a word of English. I decided the only thing to do was hand some money to the ticket conductor and let him take what he needed."

"There's nothing wrong with that."

"Wait for it," she told him, "you haven't heard the worst. I opened my coin purse and gave it to the man standing beside me. I made gestures that he was to pass it along because there was such a crowd I couldn't get near the conductor."

When she paused, Ross gave her a sidelong glance. "You've got me dangling—what happened then?"

"Well, the first man stared at the purse as if he'd never seen one before. Then the man next to him said something in Finnish and dug down in his pocket to fish out some change. Before I could stop him, he dropped a coin in my purse. Then his friend turned to give me the strangest look before he dropped in some money, too, and passed the purse to another man across the aisle. The conductor came along then and snatched it away from him. He said something in a dreadful tone of voice when he handed it back to me. I guess he thought I was begging or . . ."

"Soliciting?" Ross put in, trying to keep a straight face.

Her cheeks flamed as she nodded. "I figured that out later when those two men followed me off the streetcar. I was getting desperate when I saw you coming along."

His chuckle was reassuring. "Never mind.

You've probably made their day. All those things they've read about loose American women have come true, and they'll regale the audiences at the local tavern tonight." He drew to a stop at a traffic light and turned to look at her. "Exactly how long have you been in Finland?"

"Just overnight. I came in on the train from Turku yesterday."

"As I remember, that's a slow train . . . practically a blood brother to the Long Island Railroad."

"The slow-motion express. Believe me, I'll find another way when I go home."

"When will that be?"

His uncaring tone showed he was merely making conversation. After hesitating, Lynda replied just as casually. "Not long. I need a day or two at the Arusha plant—then perhaps another day to see what the independent Finnish artists are doing in ceramics. . . ." She broke off as he waited for a turning car. "That's enough about me . . . what are you doing here?"

For a moment she thought he looked annoyed by her curiosity. Then he said, "Strictly business. My firm arranges conventions and international trade gatherings."

"Then you've been to Finland before?"

If he was bothered by her persistence, he kept it from his voice. "Not too often, and only long enough to check a couple of hotels and fly out a few days later." He slanted a grin at her. "Hardly an expert on the country."

"At least you can find your way around."

"I just have a good sense of direction. The fact that I was taken on a tour of the Arusha plant a couple days ago has nothing to do with it."

"Now the truth comes out. But why were you touring a china factory? You don't look like the type."

"I'm not sure whether that's a compliment or not." He waited until they were safely past a streetcar before heading into a section of the city where apartment houses thinned to single-family dwellings on small, well-kept plots.

"A man who collected glass or porcelain would have mentioned it before now," she told him absently. "Offhand, I'll bet yours was a VIP tour. Am I right?"

He looked slightly discomfited. "Only because I'm arranging a fairly good-sized legal convention here next spring. Nothing personal."

Lynda found herself liking his self-effacing comment, even if she didn't really believe it. His manner showed that he was well accustomed to making decisions in a position of responsibility.

"Arusha's only a little farther along here. The company's right on the water . . . Bay of Finland," he added when she looked puzzled. "How are you going to get back to town when you're finished? You'd better have them call a taxi for you," he went on, without waiting for her reply. "Out in this part of the city, the people who speak English might be pretty thin, and considering your . . ."

"Fluent Finnish?"

He nodded. "You'd better make allowances."

His grin made him look younger. Lynda let her gaze dwell thoughtfully on his formidable length behind the steering wheel.

Evidently he was paying closer attention than she thought. "Now what's bothering you?" he asked abruptly.

"I was trying to decide your age . . . if you must know." She was too flustered to think of a quick evasive answer.

"Good Lord!" The words exploded with a masculine snort. "And I thought it was something important." There was a significant pause. Then he shot her a sideways glance. "Thirty-one on my better days. Now, about the taxi . . ."

She drew herself up, unwilling to be thought completely incompetent. "Thanks, but I'll be all right. After all, I did manage to get this far and find the only American on the block. Amy Vanderbilt might not approve of your picking me up, but it was a case of sheer necessity."

"If we're being honest, I should point out that *I* was the one who was picked up. . . ."

"I take it back . . . you're not a gentleman, or you'd have ignored that." Her glance was level. "Believe me, I don't make a habit of it."

"Stop worrying—I didn't think you did," he replied. "Incidentally, that's the Arusha plant down there in the next block on the right."

Lynda was happy for his change of subject. She leaned forward to get a better look at a complex of modern factory buildings with smokestacks towering over the roofline. "I didn't dream it was so large! It looks like a small city. I hope somebody speaks English at the gate."

"They do. You'll find some other surprises when you start touring the place. I know I did." Ross signaled and pulled up by a low building with a sign in Finnish, Swedish, and English which proclaimed that it was the main entrance for the Arusha plant.

Lynda located her purse when the car rolled to a stop and found herself wondering whether to shake hands with him or try a more casual farewell.

He solved the problem for her. "Before you go, I have a proposition I'd like you to hear. Since I've shed my gentlemanly image, perhaps I can even indulge in a little blackmail." He kept the motor running as he spoke.

"Blackmail! What on earth do you mean?"

"Don't look so alarmed. It's nothing serious. I was just wondering if you'd do me a favor and have dinner with me tonight. The city fathers have scheduled a civic banquet at our hotel. When they sent my invitation, they thought I had a wife in tow."

"And you haven't?" Lynda was watching him carefully.

"No wife."

"No wife in Finland?" she asked, leaving no room for misunderstanding.

"Not in Finland, nor anywhere else." His glance

was quizzical. "I didn't think most women cared nowadays. Or do I read the wrong books?"

"I don't know about 'most' women," she advised him, "but I like to know the ground rules."

"I'll concede the point."

Lynda's eyes narrowed. "But you're not convinced of the necessity?"

"Let's say I'm not used to furnishing references for a dinner date. Especially a civic banquet, for God's sake."

Lynda subdued a gurgle of laughter. It was blatantly clear that Ross hadn't needed any references other than his rugged good looks to attract feminine companions during most of his thirty-one years. She remembered his scowl when she'd first approached him on the crowded street corner, and grinned inwardly. Probably her reticence now was pricking a small hole in his masculine ego.

The protracted silence between them made her risk an upward look. Her glance collided with his unwavering one. Just like a cobra and a mongoose, she thought, and there was no doubt about the role she'd been accorded.

"Dinner is at seven," Ross finally announced tersely. "That all right with you?"

"Seven will be fine," she said.

"I'll be tied up at a reception earlier or I'd suggest cocktails. It would probably be better if we met in the lobby. Give that conscience of yours a rest." He was still watching her closely.

She nodded again but felt her temperature rise.

Awkwardly she reached behind her and opened the door with a sense of relief.

Ross waited until she was beside the car. "Until seven, then."

She nodded and then clutched the door as he reached to close it. "Wait a minute . . . what do I wear? Long skirt . . . cocktail dress?"

"I'll leave it to you. A navy-blue suit is the best I can do for the occasion. That's why I'm taking you along. When I have a beautiful brunette on my arm, nobody will give a damn if I wear sandals and a sheet." He waited for her to slam the door and made a U-turn toward the center of the city.

He didn't bother to look back. Lynda was sure of that because she stared after the car hoping that he would, until it turned out of sight. After that she wondered why she'd given in so meekly. She should have told him that she had no intention of having dinner with him . . . that a civic banquet sounded duller than summer reruns on television. Not that she had to worry about those in Helsinki. Finnish hotelkeepers didn't believe in spoiling their guests with amenities like television; a tiny radio was the best they offered.

Lynda turned and walked toward the main gate of the porcelain plant, but her thoughts remained annoyingly with the man who'd just driven away. Why not face it, she told herself finally. Probably she would have accepted Ross's invitation if he'd asked her to a snack of snails, shark's fins, and pickled eels. Then she grinned as she realized that, in

Finland, pickled eels might well be on the menu. She'd just have to wait and see.

At promptly seven o'clock that evening, she emerged from the elevator into the modern lobby of her hotel. A throng of businessmen was clustered around the reception desk, but several looked up from registering long enough to note her long white pleated skirt topped by a lipstick-red chiffon blouse. If their expressions were anything to go by, the ensemble was a rip-roaring success. One of the onlookers even started toward her to express his admiration in a more direct fashion, when Lynda felt her elbow taken in a firm grip and heard a familiar deep voice beside her.

"I was trying to get your attention from the corner," Ross said, looking well groomed in another dark suit and immaculate shirt. "Then I saw I'd better come and stake a claim before there were complications."

"Not as far as I'm concerned," she said, glad that the young man by the hotel desk had turned back to his registering. "I spent the afternoon speaking basic English in words of two syllables or less. I'm sure the people at Arusha were as delighted to call it quits for the day as I was." As he gestured toward two chairs in the corner of the contemporary lobby, she asked, "Do we have time to sit down here before dinner?"

"I think so . . . I peered in the ballroom a few minutes ago, and the crowd's still gathering. If we go in now, some of our hosts will feel obliged to make conversation, and it'll be more basic English and charades. Besides, a friend of mine wants to join us for a drink. Raoul's a French citizen, but after working on American projects for ten years . . . he's afraid to stay in Paris with his accent." Ross beckoned to a waiter who emerged from the bar opening off the lobby. "What will you have?" he asked Lynda after getting the man's attention.

"Gin and tonic, please . . . without much gin."

Ross nodded and gave the order to the waiter, adding a Scotch and soda for himself. When the young man had returned to the bar, Ross leaned back in his chair and surveyed her calmly as she perched somewhat tensely on the edge of hers. "I like your outfit," he commented. "Maybe I've been missing something by not hanging around street corners before."

The corners of her lips twitched. "I'm sure I have. . . ."

"From what I saw of the male reaction at the reception desk, you don't have to walk as far as a street corner."

Lynda shifted to a more comfortable position, although her expression was still wary. "You're being awfully complimentary suddenly. Either you've mellowed over the afternoon or you're getting set to tell me that my dinner partner will be fresh off the boat from Stockholm."

"Would that be bad?" He watched her wince before taking pity on her. "Sorry—I couldn't resist. You can put away your phrase book for the night. Raoul and I will tuck you safely between us." He broke off as the waiter returned with their drinks and put them on the table. "What shall we drink to?" Ross went on when they were alone again. "Street corners or basic English?"

Lynda gave him a speaking glance as she clasped her icy glass. "I was wrong—you haven't mellowed at all."

"Then I'll behave. Cheers!" He extended his drink in mock salute and took a swallow. "It's been a dull afternoon, and you rise so beautifully to the bait." When she lifted an eyebrow without commenting, he continued calmly. "It won't do you any good to give me the cold and stony, because you're going to need my help on the menu later on."

"I meant to ask you about that . . ." she began, only to be interrupted by a well-dressed man in a gray suit who drew up beside Ross's chair. He was of average height, slim with straight black hair and an aquiline nose that gave his face a haughty expression until she noticed dark eyes which were brimming with laughter as they looked down at her.

"I *knew* that there was a reason for coming to this benighted banquet with Ross tonight," he announced. "Allow me, Mademoiselle Garrett." He reached for her hand and held it expertly. "I'm Raoul Bonet . . . delighted to meet you." His head turned. "Ross, my friend . . . why didn't you tell me that Lynda was so . . . so . . . *charmante*?"

"I spent a good three minutes satisfying your curiosity, and you damn well know it," Ross cut in. "And you can dispense with your Continental hand-holding routine. Raoul occasionally forgets that there is a girl waiting for him in Paris," he advised Lynda. "She's been waiting a long time . . . and has my complete sympathy."

"Oh, that—it's a family thing . . . nothing binding," Raoul assured them, perching on the arm of Lynda's chair. "Marie and I believe in making sure before tying the knot."

Lynda started to laugh, and his face drew down comically. "I've said something funny?" he asked.

She shook her head, her shoulders still shaking with amusement. "Sorry . . . I've never heard a Frenchman with a southern accent before."

His thin cheeks creased as he beamed down on her. "Oh, that! *Incroyable* . . . no? I worked in Atlanta for two years. My mother takes to her bed and orders the *tisanes* when I go home to visit these days."

"Your mother does no such thing," Ross said, finishing his drink and standing up. "I should have warned Lynda that you're an appalling liar, as well."

"But charming . . ." Raoul said, getting to his feet, "and a public-relations genius. I would not listen to his insults," he confided to Lynda, "except that his company is one of our better accounts and I can't afford to give him the set-down he deserves. Must we go in to dinner already?" he asked as Ross checked his watch.

"We'd better," the other said, "or they'll pitch us out in the street."

"Since you're one of the honored guests, I doubt it," Raoul commented wryly. He turned to take Lynda's arm as she put her drink down and stood up. "Fortunately, I'm not at all important, so I can talk to you. Afterward, we can leave before the speeches start, and I will show you a restaurant in the park with a French singer."

"Lynda is *my* guest," Ross told him in a no-nonsense tone as they strolled toward the end of the lobby. "If I have anything to say about it, she will sit between us, and afterward, you can damn well find your own date."

His firm words didn't have any effect. Raoul waved them away with a Gallic gesture. "The trouble with Ross is that he's too serious," he told Lynda as if the other man was across the room instead of walking beside them. "He'll be old before his time. *Vraiment.* I've done my best to lighten the load. . . ."

This was received with a snort from Ross and laughter from Lynda.

"You don't believe me?" Raoul pressed for reassurance.

"Oh, I believe you," she put in, trying to subdue her smile.

"Then you're a bigger fool than . . ." Ross started to say to her, and realized that he was hardly being diplomatic. He broke off and captured her wrist as they approached the doorway of a crowded ballroom. Three people hovering by the entrance were the last remnants of an official receiving line, and they beamed as the latecomers appeared.

"Ross!" A young woman who resembled a high-fashion model held out both her hands to greet him. Her pale gold hair was brushed back from a narrow face with elegant slanting cheekbones, and a black jersey gown clung to her reed-slim figure. "I was beginning to despair . . ." Her glance passed on to the other two, and her voice rose in surprise. "Raoul . . . and Miss Garrett. I didn't realize you two knew each other."

"But of course," Raoul said with a faint bow. "Lynda and I are old friends."

"Miss Garrett's with me, Margareta," Ross said decisively. "It didn't occur to me that you two had met."

"Just this afternoon," Lynda said, feeling that she should make some sort of response. "Miss Sundstrom showed me around the Arusha plant."

The Finnish woman had recaptured her poise by then and let her smile encompass all of them as she said, "I work for the company part-time. They call me in mostly when there are distinguished foreign visitors and buyers. Like you three. . . ."

Give the woman A-plus for effort, Lynda thought. Only Raoul and Ross fit in the hostess's "distinguished" category; she had been strictly business when escorting Lynda through the plant, evidently saving her melting manner for civic banquets.

Margareta was still playing at her role. "Miss

Garrett, let me present Timo Mäki, head of the Scandinavian Industrial Development Council." She indicated a tall, partially balding man in a dinner jacket who had just finished shaking hands with Ross and Raoul. "Miss Garrett is a buyer of porcelain from New York and a guest of Mr. Buchanan's." The last was added as if to explain to the official just what a lowly creature was doing on such exalted premises.

Fortunately, he didn't appear to hold any of the Finnish woman's reservations. "I am delighted to meet you, Miss Garrett," he said in a pleasantly accented voice. "I hope you are going to enjoy your stay in this part of the world."

Before Lynda could do more than murmur a response, Margareta Sundstrom was bringing up a tall man who boasted Nordic features and rumpled fair hair. With his broad shoulders and barrel chest, he would've looked more at home felling trees for relaxation than wearing a dinner jacket at a civic banquet. "This is Birger Lindh, Miss Garrett."

Lynda smiled and interrupted her. "We met this afternoon. It's nice to see you again, Mr. Lindh."

"Exactly my thought," he said, smiling in response, his pale blue glance warmly approving as he surveyed her trim figure.

"I didn't know you two had met," Margareta said, not bothering to disguise the feline quality in her tone.

Birger Lindh explained when he saw politely inquiring looks on the men's faces as well. "Lynda was visiting the Arusha design center when I dropped by to check the exhibit today."

"How nice . . ." the Finnish woman purred. "Then Miss Garrett will be sitting among friends. Birger, I know that you'll look out for her and Raoul. Ross has to be at the official head table. Oh, dear!" She grimaced prettily. "The chairman is beckoning to us now. I'll go along and help with the introductions."

"Exactly as I surmised," Raoul said, nodding. "Mr. Lindh . . . if you'll lead the way—Lynda and I will be on your heels." He took her hand and started to urge her in the Finnish designer's wake.

"Damn!" Ross muttered. "This wasn't what I planned at all." He gave a despairing glance over his shoulder toward the head table, where Margareta stood waiting.

"It's all right," Lynda said, aware of his obvious chagrin. "Maybe later . . ."

"Most certainly later."

"Come on, Lynda, we're attracting attention," Raoul urged her cheerfully. "Nobody can eat until we all sit down."

"All right . . ." She cast an apologetic glance at Ross and moved off toward a round table where Birger Lindh was standing.

Ross remained where he was until he saw her seated, and then, frowning, made his way to the head table.

During the course of the elaborate banquet that followed, Lynda found that her worry over pickled eels was totally unnecessary. There was some sort of a raw-fish appetizer which she politely moved around on her plate, but after that there were so many good things to eat that she had trouble choosing. The main course was roast of reindeer served with a tart relish of lingonberries, and the fish course which preceded it featured sole nestled in an unusual cream sauce dotted with caviar.

As they ate, Raoul managed the conversation with effortless ease at her right hand, and at her left, designer Birger Lindh accomplished his host's duties with flattering attentiveness.

"I didn't think civic banquets were in your line of work," Lynda told the tall Finn when there was a lull between courses. "Most of the artists and designers I know at home are terribly antisocial."

"You mean they stick to their own group of friends rather than cultivating the town fathers," he said, getting to the heart of the matter. "You forget that ours is a small country. We need every international contact we can develop for our economy. It helps keep our government stable, and that's important, when you consider today's inflation and skyrocketing wage demands." He smiled. "Even to people like me. Part of my free-lance income is from Timo's Development Council."

Lynda's expression cleared. "I hadn't realized. When I met you at the porcelain factory . . . I thought you were on the permanent staff."

He shook his head. "Just one of my accounts. I travel a great deal, so I'm able to advise Arusha on what the international competition is doing in porcelain."

She leaned back as a waiter deposited a slice of whipped-cream torte in front of her. "You don't have anything to do with sabotaging your visitors' waistlines, do you?"

"Not generally. I just check the models in our tourist ads and travel promotions." His artist's eye ran over her quickly. "Besides, you haven't any worry on that score. Ross must have told you that."

"We haven't gone into it recently," she hedged.

"I suppose he's been busy." Birger gave a brooding glance toward the head table, where Margareta was keeping Ross captive with her conversation. "The budget on the international trade gathering he's arranging for next spring has every businessman in Scandinavia already counting the profits."

"Well, Miss Sundstrom seems to be doing her part on behalf of the hometeam," Lynda observed in a carefully level voice.

Birger's knowledge of English wasn't good enough to catch the underlying nuances of her remark. Raoul, however, didn't miss a thing. His eyes gleamed with amusement as he said, "Her behavior is most commendable. Ross must appreciate it."

"No doubt." Lynda picked up her dessert fork and concentrated on the food in front of her. It was disconcerting that Raoul had noticed her anger; even more annoying that she had reacted so strongly in the first place. It had to be the result of a tiring day, she told herself. Certainly there was no other logical reason; Ross Buchanan was practically a stranger. If a day's acquaintance prompted such an absurd course of action, she'd better nip their friendship in the bud.

"You're not eating your dessert." Raoul was keeping his attention on her as Birger spoke to some Finnish business associates across the table. "Would you rather have something else? I'll ask a waiter . . ."

"No . . . no, thank you. This is fine." Lynda made an effort to take another bite of the rich cake and then put her fork down. "I've just had all I can eat." Suddenly the hubbub of conversation and the soaring temperature caused by so many people in the big room made her feel limp. She pushed her plate back and shook her head when a waiter tried to refill her wineglass. "Do you think anybody would mind if I left now?" she murmured in a low voice to Raoul.

"I don't believe so. The after-dinner speeches go on and on at these shindings." He dropped his napkin on the table and leaned across her to get Birger's attention. "Lynda's still feeling the effects of jet lag. You'll excuse us, won't you?"

The designer's face immediately took on a look of concern. "Of course. I hope you'll feel better in the morning, Lynda." He half-rose as Raoul pulled out her chair. "You're coming back, aren't you?" he asked the Frenchman as they prepared to leave.

"Well . . . I . . . er . . . wasn't sure." For all his glib manner, Raoul obviously was caught out.

"It wouldn't matter," Birger murmured, "but

Timo especially wanted you and Ross to have a word with him afterward. He has some new proposals that he thought would interest you."

Lynda interrupted before the other man could think of an excuse. "There's no reason for Raoul to leave now. I can certainly find my way to the elevators alone," she went on, ignoring his chagrin. She managed a bright smile that encompassed both of them. "I'll see you soon, I'm sure. And Raoul . . . thank Mr. Buchanan for me."

She kept her glance carefully averted from the head table as she threaded her way swiftly to the doorway of the big room. The coatroom attendant stumbled to his feet as she appeared, saying something in Finnish that had a question mark at the end of it. She smiled, shook her head, and went on without pausing. As she reached the cool air in the outer hall, she took a deep breath and slowed her pace. Even so, her heart was still beating rapidly as she walked through the crowded lobby and headed for the elevators. When she finally stood waiting for an empty one, she summoned courage to look over her shoulder. There was only a young couple strolling slowly toward her; ridiculous to think that Ross would have disrupted the whole head table to come in pursuit!

Lynda's lips tightened as she kept her mind a careful blank, refusing to wonder whether the feeling that flooded over her was disappointment or relief.

By the time she had reached her room and undressed, her near-panic had disappeared. She ran water for a bath, recalling that women's magazines always touted the relaxing therapy of warm water. She frowned when she remembered that she'd already had a warm bath a few hours before, and *it* hadn't done much for her peace of mind. She was still debating whether to turn off the faucets when a knock sounded on her hall door.

Lynda tightened the sash on her cinnamon nylon robe and went to answer the summons, wondering what the floor maid had forgotten this time. It had already taken the girl two trips to turn down the bed and replace the towels. By now she was probably bringing extra soap.

A glimpse of Ross's annoyed expression as he stood in the hallway made Lynda realize that she was wrong again. Her first impulse was to close the door quickly and pretend that his looming masculine figure wasn't there at all.

Ross must have caught a glimmer of her feeling, because he simply put his hands at her waist, hoisting her aside like a bothersome umbrella stand as he stepped across the threshold and unhurriedly closed the door behind him.

"What in the dickens do you think you're doing?" Lynda got out when she recovered from her surprise. "You've an unholy nerve if you think you have the right to break in here and—"

"Lower your voice," he commanded. "I'd just as soon the whole hotel didn't overhear."

"Then I suggest you leave." She swept around him and reached for the door again. "That's the easiest solution."

His fingers clamped over hers, making it impossible to turn the knob. "I'll go in a minute. The banquet isn't over, and I'm due back. . . ."

Her eyes widened in surprise at that statement. Then she remembered his preoccupation with the elegant Margareta, and her temper flared again. "Well, you needn't have left on my account—I certainly didn't expect you to."

"Right now, I think I was a damned fool to have bothered," he told her with unflattering logic. "I don't know why I ever harbored the notion that you couldn't take care of yourself." He pulled his hand away and stared down at her in unfriendly fashion.

Lynda swallowed, uncertain of her next move. It occurred to her belatedly that her manners left a great deal to be desired. And from the ominous tone Ross had used, he concurred heartily. His broad shoulders seemed to fill the narrow hallway, and she took an involuntary step backward. "I'm sorry." Her words came out with difficulty. "I didn't mean to be so . . ."

"Combustible?" For the first time, there was a trace of humor in his voice.

Her lips curved slightly. "You could call it that."

"I'd say you had some cause. Being abandoned after a dinner invitation would try most women's patience. That's why I came along to apologize. And I didn't want to do it in the middle of the hall."

"You could have told me." There was a dangerous glint in her eyes still.

"The hell I could. You weren't about to listen." He leaned against the wall while he surveyed her flushed face. "You wouldn't have opened the door in the first place if you'd known I was on the other side. Admit it."

"I'll do no such thing. Next you'll be advising me of my rights." She put out her hands in protest. "Could we please start over again? I've just opened the door . . ."

"And invited me in?"

She shook her head and tightened the belt on her robe. "Hardly . . . I'm not dressed for entertaining." As he started to chuckle, she added warningly, "You're on the thin ice again."

"Okay . . . I'll behave. It's the least I can do after the way I've treated you tonight. I'm not sure of my plans for the next few days, but I'll see if I can make up for this."

"It really isn't necessary," she managed to say in a light tone, thinking a "duty date" was scarcely flattering to a woman's ego. "You've made a nice apology—that's all you came to do."

He continued to stare at her, and the silence between them became so heavy that it was almost tangible. Then he shook his head as he took a deep breath and moved toward the door. Lynda remained motionless, although her heartbeat was making so much noise in her ears that she could hardly hear the running of the bathwater a few feet away.

She *did* hear Ross's sudden indrawn breath, however, and saw the look of determination that came over his face as he turned in the doorway and reached out for her. The next moment she was hauled tightly against his tall length as he bent to kiss her. His movement was accomplished with such expert ease that there wasn't any time for resistance on her part. Instead, she responded instinctively and molded her body to his.

It was a full thirty seconds later—after his mouth had hardened possessively—when she remembered where she was and brought her hands down to his chest to push herself away.

Ross let her go reluctantly. He watched her straighten the lapels of her robe with trembling fingers. "I won't apologize," he said finally in a rough voice, "because I didn't have that in mind when I came up here."

"You'd better go. . . ."

"I know." He rubbed the back of his head. "I must be cracking up . . . I hear the strangest sound. . . ."

She stared up at him, puzzled. Then her eyes widened in horror. "Oh, Lord! My bathwater . . . I forgot all about it." She fled toward the bathroom.

Ross grinned and took a step as if to follow her. Then he looked at his watch and swore softly.

When Lynda came back into the hall a few minutes later, he had gone.

Chapter Two

As far as Lynda was concerned, it was an abrupt and thoroughly unsatisfactory leave-taking. Other women might take such a parting as a matter of course, but the memory of that unsettling embrace caused her to spend the next two days vainly looking for Ross's form each time she went through the lobby of the hotel.

The third morning, it was time to head for the Arusha plant again and drop off her final purchase order. By then, she was sufficiently conversant with the Helsinki tram system that the downtown transfer held no terrors. There was a faint chance that history might repeat itself, however, and she walked an extra block by the rail station in hopes that a familiar sandy-thatched head might appear among the pedestrians.

A crisp wind was blowing, but the day was sunny and the patches of sky glimpsed between office buildings were almost cloudless. Shoppers ambled at midmorning speed, content to enjoy the spring weather while they had the chance.

Lynda paused to admire an outdoor flower display and watched as the vendor wrapped a bouquet of daffodils in a cone of flowered paper, attaching a string handle to the top so that the package could swing from a customer's wrist like a brightly patterned umbrella.

Lynda moved on. There were things to do, she told herself as she walked to the tram-boarding zone. More important things than buying flowers or mooning over an elusive man who obviously wasn't trying to find her.

Resolutely she boarded the Arusha streetcar when it finally came along, and sat down in a single seat at the side. From the center of town to her destination she tried to concentrate on her job, wondering whether she had ordered sufficient quantities of stoneware and earthenware for the coming seasons. There was also the question of whether she had made the proper decision in purchasing Arusha's new ovenproof line rather than a Swedish competitor's.

From the pleased look on Birger Lindh's face when she finally gave him her purchase order at his office in the design section, there was no question in his mind.

"You won't regret this," he said, tapping his finger on the paper. "That pattern will be a sellout as soon as your customers see it."

"It'd better. Otherwise my career will consist of dusting china rather than ordering it." She bit her lip as she considered that possibility, and then decided there was no use dithering. "I'll buy a rabbit's foot when I go back through town."

"There's no hurry. Sit down and have a cup of coffee with me." He gestured her toward a modernistic leather chair by his desk. "I need a chance to practice my English."

"Your English is practically perfect now," she assured him as she sat down, "but I could use some coffee. It's a long ride out here."

"Faster than some of those cross-town taxi rides in Manhattan at the rush hour. I thought I'd go bankrupt from the fare before I arrived at the Hudson River."

"I thought the same thing this morning when I saw my bill for breakfast," she countered.

"Ah, that's different. The prospect of tourists and their traveler's checks are the only things that get Scandinavians through the long, cold winters," he said with a broad grin as he reached for a battered aluminum coffeepot on a hot plate behind his desk. Lynda was amused to discover such a relic tucked among the magnificent ceramic pieces on display around it. Birger, unaware of the paradox, rummaged for two Styrofoam cups in a drawer.

"Your new line?" Lynda asked, gesturing toward the percolator as he poured a steaming cup for her.

"What? Oh . . . this." He chuckled as he put it down and took his own cup to his desk. "One of our competitor's products, I'm afraid. About twenty years ago."

"It doesn't matter, the coffee's very good."

He nodded and inspected her over the rim of Styrofoam. "Speaking of food, I was sorry you left the banquet so early the other night. Nothing wrong, I hope?"

"Not really. I was a little tired, and I didn't think anyone would mind if I skipped the after-dinner speeches. Especially when they were in Finnish."

"Oh, no, all of us sympathized and envied you—if the truth were known." He rubbed his cheek absently with his cup. "Ross acted a little upset when he came over to talk with Raoul."

"I'm surprised he found time." Lynda kept her tone casual. "The last time I looked at the head table, he seemed occupied with the people around him."

Birger didn't bother being diplomatic. "You mean Margareta?" he asked bluntly, and when she didn't answer, he went on, "That's just her way. If there's an acceptable man within reach, it's a personal challenge." His lips twisted as if the coffee had suddenly become distasteful. "She'll never change, and I got tired waiting."

"I . . . I don't quite understand."

His aloof Nordic face softened. "No reason you should. We were engaged for a few months, then we broke it off. The parting was . . . what's the word . . . amicable."

"I'm sorry." She tried to think of something else to say and couldn't.

He didn't appear to notice. "I was the one who brought the subject up. Just in case you felt Ross's attention was straying that night. Margareta can be pretty overpowering."

"Heavens, I hardly know the man," she said defensively. "It was just a casual dinner invitation. Hardly a romantic tête-à-tête," she added, starting to smile.

"You *did* have plenty of chaperons," he said, grinning in response. "From the way Ross talked to Raoul, though, he wasn't taking your disappearance calmly. Did he find you eventually?"

"Yes." The monosyllable was casual enough, but she couldn't stop the surge of heat that flooded her body when she remembered the circumstances. She could only take another swallow of coffee and attempt to hide behind the Styrofoam cup.

If Birger noticed her heightened color, he was kind enough not to comment on it. "Good. It would be foolish to have a misunderstanding over something like that. I'm sure that Ross didn't take Margareta's actions seriously."

"Don't be too sure of that." Lynda tried to joke. "I haven't seen him since that night."

"That's not surprising—he and Raoul had some unexpected business in Stockholm. Margareta mentioned it."

Lynda felt a surge of relief that Ross hadn't been amusing himself the past two days in Helsinki with someone else. That thought lingered as she took a last swallow of coffee and stood up, putting her empty cup on the edge of Birger's desk. "Thanks for the coffee. If there's any question about my purchase order, I'll be in town for another day or so. There wasn't an available stateroom on the night boat to Stockholm, so I thought

I'd visit the park at Hameenleena tomorrow. . . ."

The door to Birger's office flew open, and Margareta burst in, holding a newspaper in front of her as she said in a high voice, "Have you seen this? My God, of all the bad luck! Saari was enough trouble before . . . now there's . . . " As she encountered Birger's fierce glare, she paused in bewilderment.

His quick "You remember Miss Garrett" was almost as quelling, and Lynda felt sorry for the other woman as she saw her suddenly stricken look. Obviously she had been speaking in English so that there was less chance of their Arusha co-workers overhearing—never dreaming there'd be an English-speaking observer at her elbow. A most unwelcome observer, Lynda decided, as the Finnish woman visibly struggled to overcome her annoyance.

"Of course I remember Lynda," she said finally. The newspaper was lowered quickly to her side and held partially behind her plaid pleated skirt. "Birger didn't mention that he was expecting you . . . I hope I'm not interrupting anything." Her voice was swiftly recovering its official-hostess guise.

"Not a thing," Lynda put in before the designer could comment. "I stopped in with my order. It's taken me this long to make up my mind."

"I'll see you to the elevator," Birger said, starting around the desk.

"Don't bother—I know the way. Good-bye . . . and thanks again." Lynda was out the door and had closed it behind her before anything more could be said.

She made her way quickly down the hall and chose to take the stairs rather than wait for the elevator. That way, she was sure to avoid another meeting with Margareta Sundstrom.

As she left the porcelain factory and made her way to the tram stop, she was still puzzling over what could have been in the newspaper that had upset the Finnish woman so much. A happening that Birger Lindh was expected to recognize just as quickly. Lynda frowned as she thought about it. Despite Birger's declaration about his broken engagement, there was still enough of a tie that Margareta hurried to his side at the first inkling of trouble.

When she arrived back at the hotel, she detoured past the combination newsstand and gift shop and bought the same morning paper that Margareta had been carrying.

The elevator was slow in coming, and she studied the front page as she waited, wishing vainly that the Finnish language didn't resist all her efforts at translation.

"I was just phoning you," said a deep masculine voice by her side. "No wonder I didn't get an answer."

Lynda jerked around, to see Ross surveying her calmly. For a moment she was torn between elation and despair. It was wonderful to see him again, although she wished that she'd had time to wash her face and comb her hair. Helsinki's public transit might be admirable, but the net result was the same as a Manhattan subway.

Ross didn't seem to notice. He was glancing at the paper in her hands with a puzzled frown. "What's going on? Are you hoping to master Finnish in an overnight cram course, or taking home a souvenir?"

"Don't be absurd." She made a protesting gesture. "Why do I always end up on the defensive when I'm talking to you?"

He grinned slowly. "Would you like it better if I said I'd missed you?"

"Well, it would be more civilized."

"Okay—I missed you, and damned if I know why," he reported in a conversational tone. "Now, what are you doing with a Finnish newspaper?"

The elevator opened beside her, and she stepped into it. "Give me an hour or two, and I'll come up with an answer."

He put out a hand to keep the door from closing. "How about fifteen minutes? I'll buy you lunch."

There was a pause while she considered. "Chamber of Commerce bash? Or a get-together for visiting Rotarians and their guests?"

"*Now* who's on the defensive?"

"Sorry." Her smile was unrepentant. "I'd love to go to lunch, thanks."

"Fair enough. I'll meet you in the dining room when you're ready." He stepped back and let the elevator door close.

Lynda set new records in changing to a fresh

blouse and redoing her makeup. Barely fifteen minutes had passed when she appeared in the archway to the hotel's sunlit dining room. She saw Ross rise from a table which overlooked a bronze patio fountain. "Sorry to keep you waiting," she said breathlessly. "I did hurry."

"That's okay—I thought you'd be longer. I cheated and ordered some coffee," he went on, indicating the cup in front of him. "We started at an ungodly hour this morning, and the lack of sleep is catching up with me." He handed her a menu. "What looks good?" he asked, after she'd studied it.

"I'll be happy with scrambled eggs and asparagus tips," she decided.

"Coffee now?"

"Please. And a glass of ice water as well. Then they won't have any doubts about our nationality."

"That's all right—we might as well enjoy ourselves today." He beckoned a waitress and gave the order, waiting until the ice water was on the table and the coffee poured before he settled back and grinned. "Damn! I should have remembered that ice water to a Finnish waitress means one ice cube per glass. I'll call her back."

Lynda shook her head quickly. "No, please. This is fine. It just looks so lonesome in there that it's funny."

"Well, at least the coffee's hot." His expression sobered as she handed the newspaper across the table. "Did you find something special in it?"

"I haven't really had time to look. You know more Finnish than I do . . . would you glance at that front page. There's a picture down at the bottom," she said, watching him unfold the paper and follow her directions. "That one with the two uniformed men standing on a dock talking to a workman."

"I see it."

"Do you know enough Finnish to figure out the caption?"

He shook his head. "I could guess at a few of the nouns, but that's all. Why?"

Lynda shrugged, trying to make light of it. "Feminine curiosity, I guess, or maybe just being nosy." As he watched her, she decided to explain. "When I was at the Arusha plant this morning, Margareta was terribly upset by something on the front page. Really upset," she went on, "and she was coming to Birger Lindh for help. You remember him . . . "

"Very well. He's called on me in New York. Sort of an unofficial ambassador, really. Being a top designer, he spends more time abroad than here." Ross lowered the paper, giving her his full attention. "What did Birger say?"

"Practically nothing. Margareta burst into the room and reeled off something about Saari being a bother before but now he was a real disaster. When she saw me, Birger started making conversation to give her time to pull herself together. After that, I left." Her lips quirked in a mirthless smile. "I had the feeling that they could hardly wait for me to close the door."

"I wonder what's going on." Ross glanced down at the picture again and then pushed his chair back. "There's no use playing games. I'll go ask the clerk at the mail desk to translate this. She speaks good English. Back in a minute."

Lynda watched him go with wry amusement. She should have known it would be a woman he was alluding to. Evidently the breadth of Ross's shoulders and his attractive rugged features hadn't gone unnoticed on his previous visits to the hotel.

He was back before she'd had time to pursue that subject or wonder just why it felt so natural to be confiding in a man who was almost a stranger.

"Well, I got the translation," he said, sliding into his chair and handing the paper across the table. "I hope it means more to you than it does to me. Apparently two members of the Helsinki police—their names are in the caption—are interviewing a crewman on a harbor dredge. The fellow was on duty when they scooped up more than mud yesterday afternoon." Ross saw Lynda frown uncomprehendingly as she stared at the picture. "It was a body," he reported baldly. "No names," he went on before she could ask, "so it probably has nothing to do with the Saari that Margareta was talking about. Incidentally, the gal on the mail desk said that Saari is a common name over here."

"Which brings us back to square one. Well, it was a nice try," Lynda said, folding the newspaper and putting it by her purse on the floor. "Thanks for your help."

"I didn't accomplish much." Ross sat back as the waitress placed their lunch in front of them. "I'll keep my ears open, though, or ask Raoul. He's more familiar with this territory than I am. Don't worry, I won't mention your part in it."

There was no more talk about the mysterious Mr. Saari during the hour that followed. Their food was tasty and attractively served, and Lynda had been in Finland long enough not to wince at the amount of the check which was discreetly put at Ross's elbow. The waitress refilled their coffee-cups as if attempting to atone and withdrew.

"Every time I see the price of anything over here, I try to remember that Finland was the only country to repay her war debt," Lynda mentioned. "I hope you can put this on your expense account—we could have been discussing a Scandinavian tour for tired department-store buyers."

"Don't worry, I'll write you off somehow. Besides, I had to get you in the proper mood for a favor I want to ask." He was amused to see her slight but perceptible withdrawal. Clearly she had been asked favors before. Ross decided that there wasn't any diplomatic way to couch his request—better to come right out with it. "There's a ship here in the harbor that leaves for Leningrad to-morrow. I'd like you to come along with me for a weekend cruise."

There was a considerable pause while Lynda simply stared at him. Then she took a deep breath and put down her napkin. "If you invite a woman to spend the weekend with you after a simple lunch date, I'm glad I didn't accept an invitation to a steak dinner." Before he could reply, she went on, "Look, Ross . . . if I wanted a casual affair, you'd be at the top of the list. You're nice-looking . . . you can be marvelous company . . . and frankly, I liked the way you kissed me the other night. But . . . . "

"Go on." His voice didn't give anything away.

"But illicit weekends don't appeal to me. All this 'new freedom' for women sounds keen, but I was brought up with a whole quiver full of puritanical inhibitions, and I'd probably go into a decline if I decided to shed them—even for a man like you." She picked up her purse and prepared to leave. "I'm sure you won't lack for company. I understand Scandinavian women do things differently. There's always the mail clerk, or maybe even Margareta. . . . "

For the first time a flicker of anger showed in his eyes. "Fixing me up?"

She flushed. "Sorry, I didn't mean to stomp on your masculine pride."

"That's all right." He leaned back in his chair, apparently not concerned with her intention to leave. "After that dissertation, there's not much left."

Her eyebrows rose in annoyance. "I thought I was remarkably diplomatic."

"But too quick off the mark. Good God, girl—if I wanted illicit love, I sure as hell wouldn't invite

you on the Leningrad cruise. The bunks in those
staterooms are worse than an upper berth on Am-
trak. They're so narrow that there's hardly room
for one person, let alone two."

"Then what *did* you have in mind . . . besides
broadening my horizons?" The last words came
out dryly. Clearly she wasn't convinced.

"I want some protection," he said without hesitation. "Margareta's been invited on the cruise, too,
and I don't want her to get any wrong ideas. Right
now Raoul is trying to arrange things so he can
come, but I'm not sure he can make it. Even if
he does, it would be best if we had another woman
to even things up. An American woman," he added
before she could make any suggestions. "And if
you're still worried, I can assure you that I've
never been attracted by group orgies, despite that
'new freedom' you were talking about. Probably
my Presbyterian upbringing." When she continued
to look undecided, he pressed on. "I can even fur-
nish references—I went to school with John Slater,
the merchandise manager for your chain of stores.
Will that convince you?"

She looked dazed. "All I have to do is go along?"

"And show enough attention to me to discour-
age Margareta. Some fond looks at dinner or over
the breakfast table should do it."

"No hanky-panky over the cabins?"

He held up a hand. "Scout's honor. Your own
key—your own berth. Be it ever so hard and narrow."

"When do we sail?"

"Tomorrow night at six."

She shook her head bemusedly. "It sounds too good to be true."

"It's true enough—don't forget to call your boss if you have any last-minute qualms." Ross stood up then and waited for her to get to her feet. "John and I fought over a blond once, but that was ten years ago. I think he's forgiven me by now."

The frown came back to Lynda's face as she paused on their way out of the dining room. "Why shouldn't he forgive you? Did something go wrong?"

"Not as far as I was concerned."

"Well, then . . ."

"I'm not sure how he feels about it these days." Ross looked amused as he took her arm and urged her forward. "You see, he married her."

Chapter Three

A feeling of excitement gripped Lynda the next afternoon as she checked out of the hotel and stepped into a cab to be driven to the pier for the Leningrad steamer.

The spell of delightful spring weather had lingered to contribute to her anticipation. A weekend cruise that started under unclouded skies was sure to be a success, she told herself, looking out the taxi window. Pale rays of sunshine still filtered through the trees on the busy Mannerheimintie thoroughfare, and later dappled the esplanade leading to Helsinki's famed flower market and wharves.

Most of the merchants in the orange-canvas stalls at the market had packed up their offerings, as early shoppers made a considerable dent in the flower and produce displays. Only vendors for household trinkets like loofah sponges and brooms were energetically holding forth, together with men selling fish from the sterns of their small power cruisers bobbing alongside the dock.

A mood of lighthearted camaraderie existed,

and Lynda noticed that a mobile coffee shop was doing a roaring business.

She was so engrossed in looking at the market-place that when the taxi drew up at a neighboring wharf, she was caught unaware. That surprise, however, was nothing compared to her first glimpse of the Leningrad cruise ship at the end of the dock. When Ross had mentioned the excursion, she had anticipated an overnight junket on a refined ferryboat—certainly not the gleaming five-thousand-ton vessel moored in front of her.

Lynda was still wide-eyed as she paid off her taxi and advised a porter of her stateroom number before lining up for Finnish immigration and customs. The leaving formalities in a small frame building didn't take long, and afterward she was directed through a back door toward the ship.

Raoul was at the end of the steep gangway, prepared to salute her on both cheeks in Continental fashion as she reached the lower saloon deck, but she managed to sidestep neatly. He looked momentarily disconcerted as he found himself shaking hands instead.

"My dear Lynda, you're in good time. We should be sailing in a half-hour. Come along with me, and I'll show you to your cabin."

"You mean you have the key?" She drew back with a frown.

"I thought it would save time for you. The stewardesses are always busy at sailing time. Ross said you'd probably like to unpack before we leave port." He gestured toward a companionway leading to an upper deck. "This way—I hope you'll like the accommodations."

Lynda's features relaxed, and she gave herself a mental poke for suspecting the worst. She followed him obediently up the stairway to the other saloon deck and down a carpeted corridor.

He pulled up in front of a stateroom door and unlocked it before handing her the key. "There you are—you should be comfortable in here. Ross and I are sharing a double cabin across the way. Incidentally, we've seen the dining-room steward and arranged for you to join our table at dinner."

She looked up, surprised. "Just the three of us?"

"No, Margareta will be there too. She and Ross are in the bar now." He glanced at his watch. "That's as good a place to watch the sailing as any. Come along, won't you?"

Lynda tried to keep her tone properly regretful. "Thanks very much, but there were so many things to do today that I'm exhausted."

Raoul's glance swept over her. "You don't look it. No matter—you *will* join us for dinner?"

"Of course." Lynda smiled as she went past him into the stateroom and started to close the door. "Thanks again for your help."

"It was my pleasure. Are you certain there's nothing else you need?"

Lynda bit back an impulse to say "Nothing that you can supply" and merely shook her head.

Raoul nodded cheerfully and turned away.

Lynda closed the door and leaned her shoulders against it for a moment as she tried to sort out her thoughts. Even a Victorian parent couldn't object to the scene so far. The stateroom was a model of Scandinavian austerity, and the most prominent feature was the narrow single berth to which Ross had already alluded. That, coupled with the key she was holding in her hand, seemed to add final approval to the expedition.

She moved on into the room and put her purse and the key on a built-in dressing table, which, along with the small blue-upholstered chair under a big porthole, completed the furnishings for her quarters. She was happy to see her suitcase tucked in a corner of the stateroom, and hauled it up on the berth to unpack her toilet articles. Further investigation of the cabin revealed an adjoining bathroom and shower with a good supply of towels. Better and better, she decided.

The sudden blast by the ship's whistle a little later made her pause in her unpacking and go over to the porthole to peer out. An ever-widening space of water between the side of the *Borg II* and the dock confirmed that the Finnish ship was leaving precisely on time.

Lynda took another look at her suitcase and then went over to slip on her beige cashmere topcoat. Suitcases could be unpacked almost anytime, but sailing from Helsinki harbor was a once-in-a-lifetime experience, and she was determined to enjoy it.

She retrieved her key and locked the stateroom door behind her after making sure that her wallet and passport were in her coat pocket. Then she walked quickly down the narrow corridor toward the stern, flattening herself along the side of the hallway when a sturdy Swedish couple suddenly emerged from their stateroom.

She reached the stern and took another stairway up to avoid the cluster of passengers leaning over the rail. On the boat deck, she found the seclusion she wanted and stood by a canvas-covered lifeboat amidships to feast her eyes on the passing scene.

The Presidential Palace and City Hall of Helsinki were still visible, along with the imposing spire of the Uspensky Cathedral. Lynda made a mental note to visit the famous Greek Orthodox church and see the icons before she finally left the Finnish capital. Then she waved to passengers lining the rails of the red overnight car ferry to Stockholm which was preparing to leave its berth and follow in the wake of the *Borg II*.

The breeze picked up and caused her to hastily tie a scarf over her hair as they passed out into the channel and headed toward the east. The sea fortress of Suomenlinna slid by on the left, the old gun emplacements which were Helsinki's wartime harbor defenses glinting in the rays of the fast-disappearing sun. Smaller islands with scaffoldings of navigational aids appeared on either side of the *Borg*'s stern as the ship increased her speed and the vibration from her engines became more noticeable. The channel marking must have been narrower than most, because the incoming freighters were close enough to make Lynda grateful for the clear weather and calm seas. When the channel markers eventually widened, she took a deep breath of the tangy air and rested her elbows on the railing. It was easy to understand why men would run away to sea, and it seemed a pity that women couldn't escape the same way.

Ross found her still staring contentedly at the calm gray waters of the Bay of Finland when he sought her out a half-hour later. "It's a good thing this ship isn't any larger, or I'd have needed a bloodhound," he said as he approached. "The only places that I haven't been are the sauna and the engine room."

"You must be joking," Lynda said, adopting his calm tone. "They don't have saunas on ships."

"They do on Finnish ships—appointments by request. And don't raise your eyebrows. Finns take their saunas very seriously. Haven't you tried the national pastime yet?"

She shook her head. "Nope. I've just looked at the picture postcards. All the talk about beating yourself with birch twigs and leaping out into the snow put me off. Besides, it's the wrong season for that sort of thing."

Ross held up his hands like a benediction. "Thanks be. I prefer this part of the world in the spring. Anyhow, you mustn't leave Finland without a sauna."

"It will come right after some icons, I promise. How did we get on the subject, anyway?"

"Beats me. I just came up to make sure you hadn't jumped ship. Raoul said you were safely aboard, but when I knocked at your cabin and didn't get any answer, I thought I'd better track you down." He watched her expressive face with some amusement. "Not to keep tabs on you; I'd just hate to have you miss dinner."

Lynda's hands flew up to her lips. "Dinner! Oh, heavens, I forgot all about it."

"You see, I do have my uses. Why didn't you join us for a drink? The scenery's just as good on a lower deck."

Belatedly she remembered why she'd been invited—a fact which had completely slipped her mind. "I'm sorry," she said slowly, "I didn't mean to offend anyone."

He took a quick glance over his shoulder before saying, "For Pete's sake, if you look like that, people will think I've been beating you. You're not on duty. I just thought the presence of another woman would show Margareta tactfully that . . ." He paused as if searching for the proper words.

". . . there was no future in her actions?"

Ross nodded. "Exactly. Without hurting her feelings unnecessarily."

Lynda thought that the Finnish woman's feelings were considerably more armor-plated than he suspected, but refrained from mentioning it.

Ross didn't comment on her discreet silence. He just looked at his watch again and said, "We'd better be moving. Dinner's in fifteen minutes, and they like passengers to be on time. There are big windows, so you won't miss anything."

Lynda nodded and fell into step beside him as they headed for the stairs at the stern. "I understand we sail through a long estuary before we reach Leningrad tomorrow morning."

"You've been doing your homework." He stood aside to let her go down. "If you want to see it all, you'll have to be up at the crack of dawn."

"I'll set my alarm," she said matter-of-factly.

His expression was quizzical as he joined her on the next deck. "If anybody had told me there was an avid tourist beneath that sleek career-girl surface, I would have said they were crazy." He held open the door leading to the stateroom corridor. "Did you check with your boss the way I suggested?" When she nodded hesitantly, he chuckled.

"Well, you said to," Lynda countered somewhat defiantly.

"I know. It's just refreshing in this day and age."

She chose to ignore that as she stopped in front of her stateroom door and got out her key. "Fifteen minutes, you said?"

Ross glanced at his watch again. "Better make it twelve. Oh, and Lynda . . ."

His voice caught her halfway into the room. She glanced back, puzzled.

"I meant to tell you . . ." He stayed by the doorway. "That gal at the mail desk in the hotel—the one I asked to translate the newspaper caption about the body in the bay . . ."

Lynda's brow cleared. "I remember."

"She caught me today when I was leaving the hotel. Said I might be interested in the follow-up to that story. Finnish authorities have finally identified the victim by his fingerprints. He turned out to be an importer named Valde Saari." At Lynda's sudden indrawn breath, Ross nodded and went on, "He had a record of minor criminal offenses."

Lynda bit her bottom lip thoughtfully. "I wonder why Margareta and Birger were involved. They aren't the kind to be associating with small-time criminals."

"It does seem strange. I would have thought those cabinet ministers at the banquet the other night were more their style. Too bad we can't ask them."

"If Margareta even suspected I'd been *this* curious, there might be another body in the bay tomorrow."

Ross chuckled. "At least, we'd better wait until we're on dry land. If you get any bright ideas in the meantime . . ."

"Then I'll tell you at dinner. Speaking of food . . ." She hesitated suggestively.

"Don't say it. I'm going. See you in the dining room."

When the gong rang a little later, Lynda had changed to a paisley print in camel and green with a soft tie neckline and was making her way forward to the dining salon.

She paused at the door to admire the walnut paneling, which provided a nice contrast to the red leather on the chairs and the immaculate white tablecloths. In the center of the room there was an elaborate buffet of appetizers, and early diners were losing no time in heaping their plates as they filed past.

Then she saw Raoul gesturing to get her attention from a table beside a wide porthole, and she smiled and moved toward him. At the same time, she saw Ross and Margareta detach themselves from the far end of the buffet and walk toward the table carrying their plates. Lynda just had time to observe that Margareta was in a slim black wool dress with a ruffled V neckline before they joined forces.

"Sorry to have stolen a march on you," Ross told Lynda as Margareta greeted her and then settled in the chair beside him. "I didn't think you'd be along for a while, and Margareta insisted she was starving."

"I decided to wait and keep you company," Raoul commented as he held her chair.

"You needn't have," Lynda said, feeling as if she'd arrived hours instead of minutes after the dinner gong. From the length of the line that was then surrounding the buffet table, it was easy to see that Scandinavians took their eating seriously.

"Nothing much else to do on this cruise," Raoul said, reading her thoughts. "After we eat, most passengers adjourn to the bar and drink cheap Russian champagne for the rest of the night."

"So speaks the man who's traveled this way before," Ross said wryly.

"Well, he's right," Margareta said, hearing a topic which could compete successfully with the pickled herring on her plate. "Although the food's very good," she added, picking up her fork again.

"Then I'm surprised you wanted to come," Ross drawled, voicing the question that was in Lynda's mind.

Margareta brushed back a strand of flaxen hair and gave him a provocative sideways-glance. "You shouldn't be. My orders are that you get the very best treatment." Her lips curved. "I'm delighted to drink champagne with you anytime, Ross, darling. And Raoul and Lynda, of course. Much more fun than staying in the office."

"There you are." Raoul pushed back his chair. "Come on, Lynda. Let's fight our way to the buffet table. Otherwise we won't catch up with those two, and it would be a shame to miss anything."

As the meal progressed, Lynda could understand what he meant. The appetizers weren't particularly outstanding, but main-course items included delectable pork loin served with the inevitable lingonberry sauce, and white salmon which tasted as good as its Pacific cousins. The accompanying Finnish bread was whole-grained and nutlike, but Lynda chose instead a portion of new potatoes, so small and round that they looked barely an inch in diameter.

When the smiling waitress suggested cloudberry tart for dessert, Lynda shook her head. "I simply can't . . . I won't want to eat again for days as it is."

"That's just as well," Raoul said when the waitress had moved to another table. "I can't remember anybody coming back from Russia recommending the food. Most of the foreigners who work there ship in a good stock of canned goods from home. Some American diplomats replenish their cupboards from London stores."

Ross nodded. "The last time I was in Leningrad, there were people in lines half a block long to buy beer at nine o'clock in the morning."

Lynda wrinkled her forehead. "Well, everybody to his own taste, but I don't think I'd bother standing in line for that. Especially at that hour."

"That's because American women are more accustomed to standing in line for a dress sale," Raoul interjected slyly.

Lynda traced a mark in the air. "Touché. I'll plead guilty there."

"Actually, you won't have to worry about standing in line to buy anything in Leningrad," Margareta said. "There are the Beriozhka shops for tourists. They only accept foreign currency, and only visitors can shop in them. Your guide will take you there just before sailing time."

"And she means 'take' literally," Ross said. "Since most of us don't have separate visas for the trip, the Intourist guide sticks closer than a Spanish chaperon. I don't suppose that will bother you two," he added, glancing at Raoul and Margareta.

Both of them admitted that they had individual visas with them.

"After all, Ross, dear," Margareta said defensively, "you can hardly expect me to spend all my time on a tourist bus, even for you. Helsinki's practically next door to Leningrad, so I come often. I imagine Raoul's in the same category."

"Well, Paris isn't that close, but I've been to Leningrad enough so that borscht and dancing bears don't excite me," the Frenchman admitted. "I'll be satisfied to stand in line at the Beriozhka for some tins of caviar."

"They'd be nice for presents, but there are different things on my list," Lynda said.

"I can make a educated guess . . ." Raoul began.

"The Hermitage museum and the Czar's Summer Palace," Ross said, cutting in. "Don't worry, Lynda, you're not alone. Every tourist feels the same way on his first trip here. I'm looking forward to them, too."

She smiled across at him, heartened by his support. Then a sudden thought struck her. "But you've seen them already—you won't want to go again. Perhaps you could arrange a substitute with the authorities."

He shook his head. "Not a chance. Don't let it bother you. I'm looking forward to a second visit. Besides, I'm not in the same league with these two world travelers," he added, observing Margareta and Raoul.

"Frankly, you surprise me, Ross," the Finnish woman told him. "You don't seem the type for a tourist cruise."

"That's where you're wrong." His voice was cheerful. "Tomorrow I'll carry a camera and stand in line for the bus with the rest of the passengers.

Don't forget, this is a vacation for me." He turned to Lynda. "Be sure you have your passport handy when we debark. The Russians take it away from you at the end of the gangplank and return it when you come back aboard."

"I hate the thought of giving it up. What if they lose it?"

"They won't. . . ."

"Yes, but what if they do," she persisted.

"Then I suppose they'd haul you off to the local pokey until your identity was reestablished." His tone showed that he wasn't taking it very seriously. "You know—fingerprints and mug shots, all the rest."

"Just like poor Mr. Saari in the harbor," she replied absently."

"Hardly. The Intourist guide at Leningrad will make sure that you don't fall off the pier. No unscheduled events are allowed." He shoved back his chair. "Who wants coffee up in the lounge?"

His abrupt change of subject made Lynda realize that she had brought the unfortunate Mr. Saari into the conversation despite her resolve not to. She looked across the table to gauge Margareta's reaction and was relieved to see the woman putting her cigarettes calmly back in her purse and brushing crumbs from her skirt as she stood up.

"I'd like some coffee," Margareta said, turning to Ross. "Especially if there's Jaloviina to go with it."

"Fair enough. We'll find out. There's sure to be

something." He stood up beside her. "How about you, Lynda?"

"The coffee sounds good." Her forehead creased in a frown. "What's Jaloviina?"

"Finnish brandy," Raoul told her, stubbing out his cigarette and getting to his feet. "You should try it once."

"Absolutely." Ross's voice dared her to refuse. "And if you don't like that . . . there are two or three other local specialties."

"Don't forget, I plan to get up early so I can see the estuary," Lynda replied, "and I don't want to hold my head every time there's a blast of the ship's whistle."

"No problem"—Ross gestured her ahead of him— "we'll send you back to your stateroom tonight before you get tipsy. Can't have you spoiling the American image any more than you have already."

Raoul was immediately intrigued. "What's Lynda done to get in trouble?"

She cut in quickly before Ross could repeat the story of her mishap on the streetcar that first morning. "It was nothing at all. Simply a lack of communication."

"Is that right, Ross?" Margareta seemed as curious as Raoul.

He nodded solemnly as they started up the stairs to the lounge. "If Lynda says so. I never argue with a lady when there's a long weekend ahead. I'd hate to start out in the doghouse."

Raoul wasn't slow to notice the heightened color on Lynda's cheeks. "From the looks of things, you might be there already, Ross," he announced smugly.

"What's this 'doghouse' you're talking about?" Margareta persisted.

Lynda deliberately threaded her arm through Raoul's when they reached the top of the stairs, and paused by the *Borg*'s lounge. "We can take a walk around the deck while Ross is explaining that, and still be back in plenty of time for coffee."

The Frenchman's face lit up in pleased surprise. "What a spendid idea! Much better than waiting in a stuffy lounge."

"Nevertheless, I'll order your coffee with ours," Ross said, sounding suddenly unamused. "It doesn't take long to get around these decks, so it will still be hot when you get back." He caught Lynda's glance while she was deciding whether or not to defy him. "Remember—there's plenty of room for two in any doghouse."

His choice of words didn't escape her. She thought briefly of the days still ahead. Of the fact that she was, more or less, his guest. And the knowledge that Ross was a formidable adversary when annoyed.

She sighed slightly and decided to be sensible. "We won't be long. I hate cold coffee," she explained for Raoul's benefit.

Ross smiled slightly, fully aware of her surrender and his victory. "Another American idiosyncrasy," he pointed out to Margareta as they turned to go in the lounge. "Cold coffee rates right along with doghouses at home. Let me tell you about it."

Lynda's lips tightened as she stared after him. So much for thinking there were no strings attached to her invitation for the weekend.

The realization that Ross Buchanan had control of every one of them in his strong lean hands didn't do a thing for her peace of mind.

Chapter Four

When the travel alarm went off at five-thirty the next morning, Lynda was surprised to see that a patchy fog had settled over the sea during the night, and the *Borg* was proceeding cautiously between channel markers off the broad estuary leading to Leningrad. The ship's whistle blasted frequently as she stood by the porthole peering out at a gray surface so calm that it scarcely seemed part of a northern sea. Just then the few ethereal glimpses of Russian mainland in the distance made it appear that the *Borg* was sailing a course far removed from the world and reality.

Lynda gave herself a mental shake; this was hardly the time to be introspective.

She went into the tiny bathroom and turned on the shower, carefully adjusting the spray before she took off her pajamas and stepped into it. There was no hurry in getting dressed afterward, she decided. Apparently the fog was going to mask everything until their arrival in the old Russian capital, so she could take her time about going out to watch their approach.

When she emerged on deck a half-hour later, bundled in a hooded nylon raincoat, she was pleased to see that the mist had thinned over some small mid-channel islands they were passing. The resulting scene looked like an oriental scroll painting, with the fog obliterating the center of the trees on the rise, leaving their feathery branches seemingly adrift above the cover. Their roots were barely visible at the waterline, and beneath them, the cold gray sea lay so still that its surface had an oiled slickness.

Lynda shivered despite the wool sweater she was wearing under her raincoat. If this was spring in Leningrad, the winter must be grim.

"Not the greatest, is it? You could have slept in for another hour," Ross said, coming up almost silently behind her. "But I knew you wouldn't, so I brought along an extra cup of tea."

She reached for it gratefully, letting the mug warm her fingers before she took a swallow. "Ambrosia! Where did you find it? I wandered by the dining room, but the doors were still locked."

He moved over to lean on the rail, his raincoat sleeve blotting the dew which glistened thickly on the teak surface. "I have an understanding stewardess who likes an early 'cuppa' herself. Unfortunately, she doesn't drink coffee, so there was no choice." He frowned slightly. "I should have asked if she had any crackers stashed away."

"This will do fine." Lynda debated for a moment whether to bring up the previous night, and decided to risk it. "The tea tastes good—I drank too much coffee last night."

"Only because you couldn't be weaned to champagne like Raoul and Margareta."

"They didn't plan to get up early," she pointed out. "What time did the party finally break up?"

"I don't know when they called it quits. I left shortly after you did—around eleven, I think."

"So my leaving early didn't make things difficult for you?" she asked carefully.

He stared at her, frowning, and then his forehead cleared. "You mean . . . because of Margareta? You'll be glad to learn that you can relax and enjoy the rest of the trip without playing chaperon. She's apparently changed tactics."

"But I thought that's why you were annoyed last night . . . when I went out on deck with Raoul. You certainly sounded like it."

Ross sighed. "Look, let's not go over it again. It's too early in the morning. I'm not at my best before breakfast."

Lynda laughed, despite herself. "Neither am I. Sorry, I should be thanking you for the cup of tea instead of acting like a marriage counselor. Let's start again, shall we?"

Ross looked relieved. "I'm all in favor of it. Especially since I wouldn't come out well in the replay." He grinned somewhat sheepishly. "Maybe you suspected that when I came bearing gifts."

She took a last swallow and shook her head. "No . . . I was too glad to have company. Imagine coming all this way and then waking up to a fog bank."

He nodded glumly as the ship slid into a thicker patch and signaled with another warning blast of the whistle. "The damned stuff certainly isn't getting any better." He pushed back his cuff to check his watch. "If it's any consolation, there's another hour before we get in port, and it's just deserted countryside along here. At least the Russians don't have to worry about anybody taking pictures today."

"You're right about that," she said, putting her empty tea mug into his outstretched hand and watching him deposit it along with his on an empty locker nearby. "Thanks, that tasted wonderful."

Ross shoved his hands in his pockets and hunched his shoulders against the cool air that funneled past the superstructure amidships. "What's on your schedule now?"

Lynda took another look at the fog swirling around them. "I don't know. What do you suggest?"

"First of all, let's go below before we freeze to the deck. There's a lounge forward with some heat in it; we can sit there until they open the dining room for breakfast. In the meantime"—he searched in his coat pocket and found a brightly colored brochure—"you can read the itinerary and decide what you want to do tonight."

She took the pamphlet and started to examine it

as she followed him down the stairs to the lower deck.

"Look out," he said, making a grab for her elbow when her feet slipped on the last step, "you'll be in sick bay before we get there."

"Sorry, I wasn't paying attention." She leafed through the pamphlet again as he opened a heavy door leading to the cabin area. "Did you read this? There's a chance to go to the ballet tonight. I can't believe it!"

He reached over her shoulder and flipped the page. "There's the circus, too, or a nightclub." The last was tacked on without any appreciable enthusiasm.

Her eyes were starry. "I can go to a nightclub or a circus anytime, but just think . . . ballet in Leningrad!"

Ross waved her onto a leather settee in the deserted lounge and sat down beside her. "Then I take it we're going to the ballet."

His wry tone didn't go unnoticed. Lynda bit her bottom lip in sudden chagrin. "I'm sorry—I didn't mean to sound overbearing. What would you prefer to do? And Margareta and Raoul?"

"I don't know about them—I didn't ask. As for me"—his slow smile appeared—"I imagine the Russian ballet will be fine. I'll go down to the purser's desk after breakfast and arrange for the tickets."

"But you don't like ballet, do you?"

"Generally I go more for pro football, but after seeing a ballet here, I might change my mind."

Lynda gave him a skeptical look. "You've had plenty of time before this if you'd wanted to," she pointed out.

"Stop being difficult. You're supposed to sit back and say 'thank you' without arguing. I sure as hell don't want to have to fight for the chance to be a martyr."

"All right. Thank you very much for taking me to the ballet. But I'll bet the next time you ask a woman for the weekend, you'll check first to see what she thinks of the Miami Dolphins."

"It'll be at the top of my list—although I lean toward the Steelers myself." His eyes narrowed. "What *do* you know about the Miami Dolphins?"

"Enough. I don't spend all my spare time going to the ballet."

Ross settled back more comfortably. "Thank God. Things are looking up."

"And I'm beginning to understand why Margareta is retreating," Lynda told him. "At least Raoul won't expect her to understand Monday Night Football."

He kept his expression noncommittal. "Damned if I know why she was so interested before. There was no reason."

"Maybe she was really interested in Raoul all along, and you were simply the red herring. Although that seems strange when she was engaged to Birger Lindh."

"She can have a different man for morning, noon, and night. Just so long as I'm not one of them," Ross said flatly. "Don't underestimate her, though. I don't think she missed that reference of yours to the man floating in the bay. . . ."

"Saari?" Lynda leaned her chin on her palm. "I didn't mean to let that slip out at dinner. It was good of you to cover up. Did she say anything later?"

"She was probing delicately after you left for bed, but then Raoul changed the subject and she forgot about it."

The sound of a chime made him yawn and stretch. "Breakfast is now being officially served. If we hurry, we can still manage to be out on deck when we come into the harbor. Once the fog thins a little, you won't want to miss the sights."

She stood up obediently. "Tell me about it. What strikes you first?"

"Sheer size. I don't know how big this port is, but the docks appear to go on for miles. It's even more impressive than Rotterdam, and that's one that takes your breath away. Of course, the port of Leningrad is the marine gateway for Moscow and the whole interior of the country, so the size isn't surprising when you think about it. Sort of a New York, Brooklyn, and San Francisco dock complex rolled into one."

Lynda's eyes gleamed with anticipation. "Let's go and eat now. If you tell me much more, I'll be so excited I won't want a thing."

"Eat heartily," Ross said, leading the way. "You'll notice that I wasn't extolling the glories of their food. Frankly, I have every intention of scrounging bread and cheese from the breakfast buffet to ensure enough calories for lunch ashore."

"I wish you'd stop thinking about calories and put your mind to positive thought on the fog."

"What good does it do to think about it?"

"I meant concentrating to make it go away."

He raised an eyebrow as they came to the dining-salon doorway. "What you need's a medicine man. . . ."

"Undoubtedly." She looked around at the passengers clustered over the long buffet table just inside the door. They were concentrating on the platters of sliced oranges and pitchers of juice at the beginning of the buffet before they turned toward the cheese trays and Finnish breads. Boiled eggs were heaped in two big bowls at the far end of the table next to the coffee urn. "From the looks of all that food, some of the rest of the passengers will be needing a medicine man, as well."

Ross waved her onto the end of the nearest queue. "Nope, they're the smart ones. They've been here before. I intend to do exactly the same thing."

"Men! How can you eat when such exciting things are happening?"

He grinned. "It's easy if you put your mind to it."

But an hour later, Lynda sensed that Ross was sharing her enthusiasm as they stood at the rail of the *Borg* as it steamed, almost wraithlike, through the occasional patches of fog that still hung over the water. Fortunately the weather had cleared enough to allow them to stare up at the unending line of ships docked on either side of the main channel. Very little was happening on any of the freighters at that early hour; occasionally one or two crew members would lean over the rail, but they seldom gave more than a second glance toward the Finnish ship.

"Most all of them are Soviet ships," Lynda reported to Ross with an air of discovery after she'd been shown the big Russian passenger liner *Mikhail Lermontov* looming high over the rest of the docked fleet.

"Just what did you expect?" Ross replied, sounding amused.

"More of a variety, I guess. Like you see in other ports."

"Well, there've been some from Poland, Estonia, and that one's from Panama," he said, indicating a vessel sadly in need of paint on its waterline. He craned his head to see the home port of a freighter just ahead. "Hey, you're in luck. That one's from Delaware."

Lynda beamed and then wrinkled her nose. "But what's that white stuff they're unloading? Everybody on deck is coated with it."

"Chemical fertilizer, I should think." Ross was giving all his attention to the freighter as they passed by. "Yes, that's it."

"And they're waving," Lynda said, enthusiastically returning the salute. "Do you think they know we're from home?"

"Well, that pink-polka-dot raincoat of yours looks more like Fifth Avenue than the Smolny

Nunnery, so I imagine they do. Those wolf whistles must sound familiar."

"All I know is that it seems wonderful to see the Stars and Stripes on that flagstaff." She blinked rapidly and mopped her lashes with the back of her hand. "The fog," she explained.

"Sure." His grin showed he knew all about that kind of fog. "It's amazing how many of us show the same symptoms when we sail into New York harbor and see the Statue of Liberty."

She smiled in response. "And I haven't even been abroad very long. I'll never make it as the seasoned world traveler."

"What's this you're talking about?" Margareta wanted to know as she came up to the rail beside them. She wrapped her brown tweed cape tighter around her slim figure and went on without waiting for an answer. "*Jumala!* What weather! We Finns wait all year for spring sunshine, and now I come to Russia to stand around in the fog." She gave Ross a negligent glance. "I should have looked for you up here in the first place . . . Americans never want to miss anything. Even if it means standing around in the cold air when there's nothing to see."

"One of our national failings," he agreed.

Lynda didn't say anything. She was secretly amused that Margareta's temper wasn't being kept under wraps any longer. Either she had given up trying to impress Ross or her interests were turned in another direction. Just then, it was hard to understand her reasoning. Ross had never looked more aggressively masculine; the raglan style of his trenchcoat emphasized the breadth of his shoulders, and the breeze had rumpled his thick hair over his forehead in a way that made him appear much younger and more approachable. Lynda stifled an urge to smooth it back and shoved her hands deep in her pockets instead.

"Another ten minutes and we're supposed to be docking," Ross commented. "Have you heard whether we're on time, Margareta?"

"I should think so," she replied, still frowning. "Hear that music? We must be near the dock. If only this fog would lift a little . . ."

Lynda narrowed her eyes to try and see through it. "Where is the music coming from? Have they scheduled a brass band to welcome us?"

Margareta's expression cleared. "No . . . no. It's a tape recording. Military bands aren't summoned for an unimportant cruise ship like this."

"Oh, I see." Somehow a taped musical welcome left a lot to be desired as far as Lynda was concerned.

"It's hardly worth the effort," Ross said, obviously agreeing with her. "They did the same thing when I sailed from Hong Kong once."

She nodded. "It reminds me of the new curate in my folk's hometown. He decided he was too busy for home calls, so he got the idea of taping his messages—even condolences for bereaved families. After a few weeks, the bishop learned about it."

"What happened?"

"The last I heard, the curate was back to paying

calls in person—only, at his new parish in Prudhoe Bay." She looked around. "You know, the weather's improving—I think the sun is trying to burn through."

"I hope so." Margareta was peering across to the other side of the ship. "They have some ships anchored over there in mid-channel, and I think our tug just came closer to that last one than he planned to. A shipwreck's all we need right now . . . my head already feels as if it's exploding every time they blow that whistle." Her gaze rested irritably on Lynda's face. "You were wise to go to bed and skip the champagne last night. I shouldn't have listened to Raoul. Frenchmen! They must be hollow inside."

"Where *is* Raoul?" Ross asked casually.

"Down consuming a tremendous breakfast." She shuddered visibly. "Nothing affects his appetite."

"Not that I've noticed," Ross confirmed, "but then, he's an old hand at drinking people under the table." At her puzzled look, he went on, "An American expression."

"I see." Patently she didn't, and waited for him to explain.

He appeared not to notice, concentrating instead on the long concrete quay which could be seen ahead of their bow. There was a Russian flag on a pole next to a low building where the martial music blared from speakers at the roofline. The pier itself was almost deserted except for three men in green army uniforms and a port official wearing a black uniform with gold stripes on the

sleeves. Each of them bore a chest full of medals.
"Even on a foggy morning in May," Lynda said,
almost to herself.

Margareta gave her an inquisitive look but
didn't comment. Ross smiled slightly. "It was the
same when I was here before. Great people for
uniforms."

"I wouldn't say that they were overjoyed to see
us," Lynda offered cautiously.

"Maybe they're unhappy about the weather . . .
or they haven't had their coffee break," Ross said.

"Or they had a fight with their wives before
they left home," she added.

"And the kids didn't get in until midnight, and
woke everybody in the block when they finally appeared," he went on.

"Makes you wonder what the country is coming
to, doesn't it, comrade?" Lynda's eyes were spar-
kling as she sparred with him.

"What *are* you two talking about?" Margareta
asked.

"We were discussing the ecstatic welcome," Ross
drawled, jerking a thumb toward the dock, where
the sober-faced officials were now watching the
berthing. A man who was sweeping alongside the
fence leading to the customs building gave the
Borg a cursory glance before going back to his
brushwork. It wasn't a speedy operation—hardly
surprising, when a closer look at his broom showed
it was simply a bunch of twigs tied together.

Some crew members of a small Soviet cruiser
tied on the other side of the pier watched without

expression as the *Borg* was made fast and two la-
borers in coveralls shifted a wooden gangway onto
the ship under the direction of the port official.
The music from the customs shed was cut off
abruptly as the docking was completed. Apparently
the civic welcome, such as it was, was officially
over.

"We'd better get back and collect our things.
Once landing formalities are completed, the tourist
buses leave promptly," Margareta said, turning
away from the rail.

"I thought you had other plans," Ross said in
some surprise. "You can't want to sit on a tourist
bus."

The Finnish woman shrugged. "It's better than
sitting on this ship. I just remembered that the
friends I planned to visit aren't coming back to
the city until tomorrow. Besides, a visit to the
Hermitage will be of some value to me. Birger was
thinking of a possible Russian border design for
Arusha's earthenware theme next year. I could see
something that would be helpful."

Lynda followed her along the deck. "That
sounds like a marvelous idea. The fashion designers have already used peasant embroidery design in
their field, but there's no reason why it wouldn't
be just as successful in ceramics."

"Wait a minute," Ross protested. "I thought
this was supposed to be a vacation for you two."

Lynda smiled over her shoulder at him. "An oc-
cupational hazard," she explained. "It's fun to be

in at the beginning of something like this—the design possibilities are endless."

"I had a few designs myself," he told her in a lower tone as Margareta led the way past the corridor doors. "And it didn't have a damned thing to do with earthenware."

Lynda paused by her stateroom and said mischievously, "But you said there were no strings attached."

Margareta was unlocking her door just down the corridor. "I'm going to hurry off the ship and make a telephone call at the customs hall. Save me a place on the bus, will you?"

"Of course," Ross said tonelessly, and watched her disappear into the stateroom. "That's great. Just great," he said, turning back to Lynda. "The way things are turning out, we might as well be going with an Elks Lodge convention. Not only that, you and Margareta will be huddled over every icon in the museum, trying to decide whether it might do for the spring line."

Her lips twitched. "You forgot Raoul."

"No, but I'm trying to. Are you sure you don't have any relatives in Leningrad that you'd like to visit, too?"

"Not a one. Scout's honor. Don't be annoyed, Ross," she coaxed. "It's been such fun, so far."

"I'm sorry." He shook his head slightly. "I didn't mean to put a damper on things. Everything will turn out fine."

She touched his wrist, drawing one shapely finger down the back of his hand. "There's always the ballet to look forward to."

He caught the finger in a firm grip and raised it to eye level between them. "Somebody should have whaled the dickens out of you the first time you started twisting men around this slim digit. You've been getting away with murder long enough."

She pulled gently but didn't succeed in loosening his grip. Somehow that didn't bother her at all. Any more than the passengers trudging past in the narrow corridor who looked with good-natured interest at a couple holding hands so early in the morning.

"If you're going to start reforming me now, we'll miss the bus," she said finally when Ross showed no disposition to move.

"And the commissars wouldn't like that." He smiled slightly and gave the finger an absent squeeze before releasing it. "All right, we'll postpone retribution for the moment. But it will take place—be assured of that. All I have to do is pick the country."

Lynda caught her breath in surprise. It was Ross's first intimation that their relationship wasn't going to be written off as soon as they docked in Helsinki once again. And typical of him that he didn't even ask what she thought about it. She glanced around the busy corridor, thronged with passengers carrying cameras and passports as they emerged from staterooms ready for a day ashore.

Hardly the place, Lynda decided, to look up at

the man beside her and say: "If that's the way you feel . . . why did you announce it here? Why now? When we can't do a blasted thing about it?"

Her expression must have given her away, because Ross had trouble keeping a straight face. "I didn't dare say anything before. You might have thrown that cup of tea at me."

It wasn't what he said—it was the way he said it that made Lynda's pulse go into double time. "I'd better get my passport," she said in confusion as she pawed ineffectually for the doorknob behind her.

"Allow me." He reached down and pushed the door open.

"You're not coming in . . ." There was the flutter of panic in her voice.

He shook his head. "Not here. Not now," he added obliquely. "I'll meet you at the gangway in fifteen minutes. Bring a coat. It might be cold in the bus."

Lynda spent three minutes stowing her passport and traveler's checks in her purse and then the next ten minutes staring out her porthole. Ostensibly she was looking at the harbor activity, but in reality her thoughts were still taken up with Ross's last remarks.

Then a look at her wristwatch made her realize that he wouldn't be delivering any more compliments if she kept him waiting.

Two stern-faced soldiers at the lower end of the gangway made her slow her pace halfway down the steep wooden steps. She glanced over their heads, to see Ross waiting for her a little farther along the pier. He smiled and gave a surreptitious thumbs-up gesture to bolster her first contact with Soviet officialdom.

Lynda decided that the frowning Russians weren't going to intimidate her, so she presented her passport calmly when the first held out his hand for it. He scrutinized the identification picture and then stared fixedly back at her for a full five seconds. She returned his gaze, unblinking. Finally he nodded, his face completely impassive as he handed her passport to the other soldier, who gave him a shore pass in return. This was delivered to Lynda without a word.

"Thank you," she said. It was a great temptation to add "Have a nice day," but she sternly resisted and simply walked on down the dock. Ross was watching her expression as she joined him, and they started toward the customs building.

"Welcome to Mother Russia," he said.

She began to laugh. "If they hope to increase their tourist business, somebody should slip in two or three men from the Honolulu Chamber of Commerce on the next grain shipment. That soldier on the gangway made me feel like a fugitive from Devil's Island."

"Maybe he's new on the job."

"Then he should practice smiling once a month. Otherwise, he'll be an old man before he's thirty. Good heavens, there's another one." She tried not to stare as they passed a young soldier standing at attention on the pier next to the bow of the ship. "Will he do that all day?"

"Probably." Ross didn't shorten his stride. "Maybe our captain was afraid someone would steal his ship while we were here."

Lynda gave a soft snort of derision before staring around her curiously. Other than a few men peering through the high wire fence bordering the dock, the adjacent area was completely deserted. The only sign of activity was by the low customs shed ahead of them, where five or six buses were parked in a wide driveway. "I know it's still early, but this place is so quiet that it's almost eerie," she said.

"There'll be more people in evidence when we drive toward town. Raoul said he'd meet us at the bus. He was going to round up Margareta on the way."

By then they had caught up with the rest of the *Borg*'s passengers, who were strolling into the customs building and passing through the deserted rooms. "Nobody's debarking officially," Ross said in Lynda's ear; "therefore, no customs."

After the thoroughness of the immigration check, Lynda gave silent thanks for that. Walking with the rest of the passengers into a big room beyond, they observed a money-changing cage in one corner and a tightly locked gift counter in another.

A few passengers were changing their currency into Russian money, but Ross shook his head at Lynda's questioning glance. "No point in it," he explained. "We won't be anyplace to use it, and you have to change it all back before you leave the country and account for what you've spent. No kopeks or rubles can be taken out."

"And the Beriozhka shops only take foreign currency, don't they?" Lynda sounded deflated. "It certainly seems different."

"It is different," Ross said levelly as he held the door for her to go into the big paved drive. "Don't try to sort things out now. You'll have plenty of time when you get home. Just keep your eyes open. C'mon, there's the English bus over there."

"What do you mean . . . English bus?"

"The sign on the windshield. That means we'll have an English-speaking Intourist guide."

"I see." She was scrutinizing the other buses. "French, German, Finnish-Swedish. Something for everybody. Or almost. What happens if you only speak Swahili?"

"Damned if I know." He grinned down at her as they walked across the roadway. "I could ask and find out."

"Don't you dare! They'd probably root around and find a Swahili guide. Then where would I be?"

"In a bus all by yourself," he stated positively. "Want to get on this one? It looks about full."

Lynda nodded and clambered aboard, returning the pleasant nod of a short and stocky bus driver before she started down the aisle.

Raoul and Margareta waved from a seat halfway back. "I'm glad you're finally here," Margareta said as Lynda slid into the empty seat across from them and Ross sat down beside her. "We were trying to keep it for you," Margareta went on in a lowered tone. "It wasn't easy."

Judging from the censorious look bestowed by two couples farther back, Lynda could see what she meant. "Thanks, it was kind of you." She leaned farther across Ross to add, "Good morning, Raoul—I'm surprised to find you here."

"No more than I," he said with a grimace which turned into a full-fledged yawn. "Margareta's to blame. She threatened me with dire peril unless I kept her company today."

"At least we'll have two experts if we want to ask questions," Ross commented. He broke off as the bus door was slammed and a short, chunky brunette wearing a blazer striped in shades of brown and a plain brown skirt stood by the driver. She tapped her finger on the microphone to see if the power was on and said, "Good morning," when the volume was adjusted. "I am Rita, your guide for the trip today." She gave them a self-conscious smile before going on in accentless English. "If I forget something, you will please tell me, because this is my first trip and I am a little . . . nervous." Only the slight hesitation as she searched for the proper word showed that her command of the language wasn't quite as good as it appeared. Her brown eyes were friendly, though, as she said something to the driver. It must have been the Russian equivalent of "Let's get going," because he nodded and immediately started the engine. Rita sat on a jump seat beside him as they drove away from the port area and turned onto a broad arterial.

Lynda peered through the rear window to see if the rest of the buses were leaving as promptly, and noted that they were following faithfully in convoy.

Rita had unearthed a memo book from her purse and started to deliver a capsule version of the city's historic past, beginning with Peter the Great, who was called to the czarist throne in 1682. There was a short deviation while she explained how St. Petersburg was founded as a "window into Europe" in 1703 before becoming the capital of Russia nine years later. She lingered longer on the Decembrist revolt in 1825 and Red Sunday in the 1905 revolution. At that point, she was interrupted by a passenger in the front seat who wanted to know the name of the river beside them.

Rita put her finger on the page to keep her place and announced that it was the Neva River. "The city was constructed on the Neva Delta," she said, keeping her other hand firmly on the microphone. "Now there are more than three million people in this area, and the city is intersected by many canals. We have more than six hundred bridges," she announced as the bus rumbled over one of them.

Lynda was trying to pay attention to the statistics as well as keeping her gaze on the bus window so that she wouldn't miss anything. When Rita was diverted by a question from the driver, she turned to Ross and said, "This is fascinating, isn't it? Seeing something new, I mean."

He nodded, his glance understanding.

"And I'm so glad the weather has improved," she went on.

"Well, at least we left the fog on the water. There's a pretty heavy cloud cover, though."

She frowned thoughtfully. "Maybe that's what makes everything seem so gray and drab. Of course, these rows of apartment houses aren't much for scenery, since they all look alike. At least the shade trees in front of them are pretty." She gestured toward the curb. "Why are people standing in a line by those strange balloonlike trailers?"

"The trailers are the beer wagons I told you about. If you look closer, some of the people have glasses in their hands."

Across the aisle Raoul shrugged and said, "Maybe they're thirsty—and there aren't any tables and chairs on street corners."

"That way you aren't disposed to linger," Ross put in, "or have one for the road."

Lynda winced at his pun. "I'm going to look at those gold domes in the distance instead. They're perfectly beautiful. Maybe the guide will tell us about them."

Rita did, but in good time. First she had to explain how the city was named Petrograd in 1914. Afterward she went into a long explanation of the revolution of 1917, when it was renamed Leningrad for the Marxist hero.

By then Lynda decided that Rita had been ordered to provide a political lecture with each episode of history, so she concentrated on the scenery outside instead. The number of people on the sidewalks increased as they approached the center of the city. Many of them stood in lines waiting for buses and streetcars, which provided most of the transportation. There were some automobiles on the streets, but surprisingly few. She had decided to ask how much it cost to buy a car in the Soviet Union when her attention was distracted by the entrance to the Leningrad Zoo. The zoo-goers crowding around the drab wooden archway were mainly older women chaperoning younger children. The youngsters were obviously delighted by the outing, and their joyful expressions made Lynda realize that she had seen few such laughing and talkative faces so far. The people were well-fed and adequately clothed, but there was little of the lightheartedness she had seen in the Scandinavian countries.

She was still thinking about it when the bus pulled up to park alongside two tall columns with strange-looking iron decorations on them.

"We are now at the Strelka," Rita announced, getting to her feet as the bus driver opened the door. "These monuments are the rostral columns which once served as landmarks for ships. Alongside is the Neva River again." She pointed to the broad expanse of gray water with a few sightseeing launches tied to a pier on the other side. "Beyond those boats," Rita went on, "you'll see the famous Hermitage Museum, which we'll visit after your lunch." Then, as she noticed that most of her audience was already on its feet shuffling toward the open bus door, she said quickly, "We will talk of this later. Five minutes for your photographs."

"Lives there a tour guide with soul so dead who hasn't said that phrase at least once. It must be the first thing they're taught," Ross muttered, standing up and looking at Lynda. "Want to get out?"

"Wouldn't miss it." She slid across to the aisle seat and glanced over at Raoul and Margareta. "Are you coming?"

Margareta wrinkled her nose. "Not until someone announces lunch."

Raoul nodded approvingly. "My feelings exactly. Explain to the guide when you go out. She's giving us a disapproving stare right now."

"You can make your own excuses," Ross told him, heading down the aisle. "Otherwise our time will be up before we even get out of the bus." A minute later, after he'd helped Lynda down the steps, he grinned and announced, "Young Rita is going back to find out what's wrong. I thought she would."

"She just can't understand anybody not wanting to see a rostral column," Lynda said, walking over to look up at one. "Okay, I give up. What *is* a rostral column? Those iron things on the sides look like baskets."

"Rostral means having to do with the prow of a ship. These were taken from some of the older ships and preserved. Years ago this place was used as a navigational aid for traffic on the Neva."

Lynda nodded and smiled as she saw him reach for his camera. "While you're taking a picture, I'll wander a bit."

He found her a few minutes later at the waist-high barricade looking across the gray river to the imposing old buildings lining the other side.

"It's more impressive at a distance. Then you don't see the neglect and the untended parts," she said.

Ross nodded understandingly. "This part of Leningrad seems as if time had passed it by. Just look at those czarist palaces and the golden domes of the imperial churches with the Neva flowing past—it might be Venice and the Grand Canal." He stared up at the sky and sighed. "Unfortunately, the weather can't compare with southern Europe."

Lynda started to chuckle as they walked back toward the bus. "The photographer's lament." Once they had reseated themselves, she turned to Raoul. "How did you square things with the guide?"

"Ask Margareta," he said, giving her a sideways glance. "The discussion was in Russian . . . I didn't understand a word of it."

The Finnish woman put her sleek blond head back against the seat cushion. "I told her that the man next to me was a mental case"—she paused to give Raoul a mocking appraisal—"and that I didn't dare leave him alone."

Raoul's eyebrows drew together. Then he burst out laughing. "And she believed it?"

"Naturally," Margareta said. "I also said you were French."

"*Merci,* you are too kind." He shrugged well-tailored shoulders. "At least, we shouldn't have any trouble having a table to ourselves for lunch."

Lynda was amused at his quick summing up. "No wonder you use him in your business," she said in an undertone to Ross as the bus started off again.

"I think he's met his match in Margareta," Ross agreed. "Oh, Lord, here comes the next round of statistics."

Their guide was pointing to her left as the bus swung into a broad boulevard. "Here you will see the Central Museum of Ethnography . . . "

"Only from a distance, I hope," Ross murmured.

"Sssh, we might miss something," Lynda said.

"I certainly hope so."

"And next to it, the annex used by the armed forces," Rita droned on, gesturing toward a brick building. "It can be identified easily by the steep steps."

Lynda obediently looked at the steep steps. Then her expression changed suddenly, and she reached out to get Ross's attention. "That tall man with the Russian in the army uniform just coming out of that building . . . "

"What about him?" Ross bent forward to see.

"Isn't that Timo something or other? The official at the banquet in Helsinki."

"Timo Mäki," he murmured automatically. "It

looks like him, but I don't know what he'd be doing there." He turned his head, "Margareta, that tall man at the bottom of the steps over there —I don't know whether you can still see him . . . yes, you can," he added. "We've slowed down to turn."

"What about him?" Raoul wanted to know, as he half-stood as well to look over the back of their seat.

"Isn't that Timo Mäki?"

"It could be." He was squinting. "What do you think, Margareta?"

She shrugged and sat down again. "Possibly. It's hard to tell. Why does it matter?"

"Just that he's supposed to be one of the most anti-Soviet citizens in Scandinavia," Ross said, frowning thoughtfully. "This is strange company for him." As he sat back in his seat, he became conscious of Lynda's hand clutching his arm and her intent profile as she stared through the window. The traffic around them cleared, and their bus started up again as he asked, "What's the matter? Is something wrong?"

She brushed her hair back with an unsteady hand. "I *must* be seeing things today. Either that, or it's reunion week in Leningrad."

He leaned across her to stare through the window, and then pulled erect again with a frown. "I don't see anyone familiar. Some friend of yours?"

Lynda bent her head so that her voice wouldn't carry. "Not really. It was Birger Lindh from Arusha. I wonder if Margareta knows he's here."

"Could be," Ross said, keeping his voice low as well. "Maybe that affair isn't in the past tense."

"Well, why in the world was he wearing a pair of dark glasses and pretending to inspect a sidewalk display of books in Leningrad?"

"Why not? How do you know Birger was pretending? Maybe he collects Russian books on the side."

"He wasn't even *looking* at the book in his hand. He was staring across the street the way we were—watching Timo Mäki on the steps with that Russian officer."

"This could be a lot of guesswork on your part," Ross pointed out quietly. "There are a hundred reasons—legitimate ones—for both of them being in Leningrad today."

"I know that." Lynda's face looked drawn and tired suddenly. "And you can call it feminine intuition or whatever you like, but there's one thing I am certain about."

Ross waited for her to go on, his eyes hooded and expressionless.

"If I ever saw a man with murder on his mind," she told him with sure conviction, "it was Birger Lindh two minutes ago."

Chapter Five

After that, the rest of the tour seemed anti-climactic.

Lynda and Ross sat quietly in their seats, ostensibly listening to Rita's commentary as the bus went on its appointed rounds before lunch. They were driven past the building housing the Kirov Ballet, shown the subway stations, and toured past the Smolny Institute, which Czarina Catherine II had founded to educate women from the noble families. Lynda observed it all without commenting, and it was hard to tell from Ross's thoughtful expression just what was occupying his mind.

Raoul had his eyes closed and seemed to be napping comfortably. Margareta's attention was fixed on a notepad she'd taken from her purse. Occasionally she would write a word or two on what looked suspiciously like a shopping list.

Ross smiled slightly as he saw her preoccupation. Their neophyte guide would be chagrined to know that her political lectures were falling, if not on deaf ears, on determinedly inattentive ones. He shot a glance at Lynda's profile as she turned to observe another of the old Russian churches, which Rita reported as "no longer functioning." Lynda's slight frown didn't come from that, he'd wager. Clearly, Birger Lindh's appearance still caused her concern. And it was hardly the kind of situation that could be easily resolved. His acquaintance with Margareta wasn't the kind to survive a question like "What's your ex-fiancé doing spying on your boss in Leningrad?" Especially if he followed it by "And what the hell's your boss doing on this side of the political fence anyway?"

Rita's monologue made barely discernible inroads as the bus turned into a large open square with a military statue in the center of it. The guide gestured toward a gigantic poster of Lenin which covered the front of a three-story building as she explained, "This decoration is still being preserved from our May Day celebration. Moscow is not the only city to have an observance on that day. The Soviet people all over—"

Her speech was rudely interrupted by a woman in the front of the bus saying, "For heaven's sake— look at the bride in that car with the white ribbons. Right over there by the statue."

Instantly the audience on the bus came to life as they watched the little drama enacted in the center of the square.

"She's getting out," another woman contributed unnecessarily, because by then all the bus passengers were at their windows. "That must be the groom in the dark suit."

"Which one?" somebody wanted to know. "There are four men in dark suits."

"The one next to her," another woman stated impatiently. "Look, the bride's walking around the statue with him. What are they doing that for?" she asked, turning back to the Intourist guide.

Rita put her notes aside to smilingly explain. "It's a Russian custom. After the marriage ceremony, the bridal party goes to one of our best-loved statues. Generally a hero of the Soviet Union. Then she carries her bridal bouquet around the statue three times."

"For luck?" a man asked.

Rita shrugged. "Of course . . . and happiness. Whatever brides wish for. Afterward she will leave her flowers at the base of the statue."

"Charming," said an elderly woman, and there was a murmured agreement as the rest of the passengers reluctantly settled down again.

It became immediately apparent, though, that they were dissatisfied with their itinerary. Rita was buttonholed by a man just behind the driver. "Frankly, little lady, I've had about enough," he told her in a kindly but definite voice. "I don't know about the rest of the bunch"—he turned to survey the approving faces behind him, and then faced the guide with more assurance—"but we'd like to postpone the sightseeing until after lunch."

Rita stared back at him uneasily. "But the Cathedral of St. Isaac should be next. We get out and visit it for an hour. It has been transformed to an excellent museum."

"Sounds fine, but my feet can't take it until afternoon. The rest of the folks feel the same," the man said firmly. When Rita glared, he simply folded his arms over his chest.

The Intourist guide hesitated a moment longer and then rattled off some conversation to the driver. He frowned, shrugged, and replied tersely. Clearly they hadn't anticipated a revolution among the passengers.

"Very well," Rita said finally, turning back. "We will have lunch if the restaurant is ready to serve when we arrive." Before she sat down in her seat, she fixed the spokesman with an annoyed glance. "I think you are a very undisciplined person."

Ross laughed. "What do you know! I would have put up money that our early lunch would lose to the cathedral."

Lynda nodded. "And Rita would say 'It is forbidden' again. They must teach guides those three English words first of all."

"Well, let's hope we don't need any Russian words to get through the lunch menu. My vocabulary's pretty threadbare."

"All I know is 'yes,' 'no,' and 'I love you.'"

"If that's the case," he said solemnly, "I hope you have an attractive waiter."

When they arrived at the appointed tourist restaurant a little later, they found that Rita had everything well under control, despite her threat that an early arrival could be disastrous. The restaurant staff was ready and waiting to usher them into the modern, mirror-fronted building.

Margareta and Raoul hung back on the sidewalk, however, and shook their heads as Rita gestured them in.

"Sorry," Margareta said, "this gentleman and I will leave you here."

"But the group must stay together at all times."

"We have individual visas," Raoul said firmly, "and we have other plans for lunch." He took Margareta's elbow as he announced to Ross and Lynda, "Probably I'll join you at the Hermitage later on. The tour bus is the easiest way to get back to the ship. My Russian isn't good enough for local transfers on my own."

"I think I'll join you at the Hermitage, too," Margareta put in. "There's no sense in wandering around it on one's own."

"Won't it be difficult to find us in such a huge place?" Lynda asked.

"Not really. There's only one main entrance to the museum, and a set route after that," Margareta said. Lowering her voice, she added, "Anything else is forbidden."

"Say no more. We understand," Ross said, nodding as the guide caught his eye and motioned for them to come in the restaurant. "We'd better go. See you two later, then."

Lynda was barely given time to echo him before she was ushered into a mirrored hallway with a cloakroom on one side. The latter was presided

over by a man wearing a white jacket and a row of
army medals on his chest. Ahead of them, a maître
d' in a dark suit gestured for them to follow, and
led the way into a large dining room crowded with
tables.

"Mmmm. Clean table cloths and cloth nap-
kins," Lynda murmured, unfolding hers when she
was seated beside Ross. "So far . . . so good. And
it looks like soup for the first course." She caught
a glimpse of a white topping in each bowl. "With
sour cream. Borscht, of course."

Ross lifted his spoon as a bowl was put in front
of him. "Borscht—of course. Sounds like a television commercial.

> "What do you eat in Leningrad,
>   Or any other Russian pad,
>   Borscht . . ."

He broke off quickly as Rita came to inspect
their table.

"Will you behave?" Lynda hissed when the girl
walked on. "You'll get us thrown out of here."

"Not another word," he promised. "At least until after dessert. You know, this borscht isn't half-
bad."

Unfortunately, the rest of the lunch didn't rate as
well. The fish course was pungent and best ignored. The beef-type stew was strong on sliced car-
rots, and the few chunks of meat bobbing among
them were of sturdy, bubble-gum consistency.

Lynda chewed hers for a while and then gave

up, deciding to wait for coffee, which was being served, European style, after the final course.

She took a sip of it and sighed.

"Still hungry?" Ross summed up her feelings immediately. He grinned slightly. "So am I. I told you that cheese sandwich I brought along from breakfast would come in handy."

"Tomorrow I'm making one of my own." She eyed the hard green apples on a plate in the middle of their table and decided against experimenting. It didn't take a medicine man to predict the effects of borscht combined with green apples. There would be no attending the ballet later if she tried *that* one. To get her mind off food, she sat back in her chair and asked Ross, "I wonder what Margareta and Raoul were going to do when they left us?"

"Probably find a decent place to eat," he quipped. Then he shook his head. "There's no telling. Raoul has spent quite a bit of time here on visits, so maybe he's calling on a friend."

"From what I know of Raoul, it will be a woman friend."

"He takes being French seriously, that's all." Ross sounded amused.

"Maybe on this trip he's settling for a bird in the hand."

"Margareta?" He shook his head slowly after thinking it over. "Not really his type. I gather she feels the same way. I'd be more interested in knowing where *she's* spending her free time. There's something about the woman that doesn't ring true."

"She could be meeting Birger. I don't think she saw him this morning, but . . . " Lynda broke off before saying in a rush, "What in the dickens was he doing skulking around?"

"You don't *know* he's skulking. Lots of people wear dark glasses without ulterior motives. Maybe the sun just hurts his eyes." He ignored her murmured protest and went on. "There could be any number of legitimate business reasons for his being in Leningrad. From what I've heard, he has connections all over—sort of like Raoul. Making a fast dollar isn't an occupation restricted to American businessmen. Most Europeans could give them lessons in it." Ross sighed as he watched Rita start rounding up people at the next table. "Frankly, I'm getting a little tired of our chaperon. Being treated like a five-year-old all day has its disadvantages."

"Too bad she didn't come over and offer to cut our meat," Lynda said, taking a last swallow of coffee. "I could have used some help."

Ross chuckled as he got up. "Maybe we'll be on our own at the Hermitage this afternoon."

"Lord, I hope so. How could we keep together going through a museum that size? The guidebook says there are over a thousand rooms and a hundred and seventeen staircases."

"Rita will find a way. She's gotten a second wind by now."

Ross was right. Rita had no sooner counted

noses on the bus and signaled for the driver to leave than she announced, "First, we shall stop at the Cathedral of St. Issac, where we *should* have stopped before lunch. Then we will go on to the former Winter Palace, or the Hermitage Museum. Our tour through the museum will last exactly two hours." She was consulting the notes in her hand. "Naturally, that will not allow us to cover everything, but we have selected the most interesting paintings and sculptures for you to see."

Ross muttered irritably. "So much for individual efforts. I hoped to spend most of my time looking at the collection of French impressionists."

Lynda frowned in sympathy. "I know. And she didn't say anything about the Fabergé eggs. Do you suppose they're on the tour?"

"We'll have to wait and see." He grimaced. "Did I say five-year-old? Make that a babe in arms."

"If she zips through the museum as fast as she does everything else, we'll be crawling on our hands and knees after two hours." Seeing Ross rummage in his film case, she asked, "What are you looking for?"

"Calories." He pulled out his cheese sandwich and broke it in half. "Take part of it. I have a feeling we'll need to keep up our strength."

An hour and a half later, Lynda wished that he'd brought a thicker sandwich. By that time, they were up on the third floor in one of the many annexes of the museum. She had given up counting rooms long before. Rita had led them up and down endless marble staircases with abandon, scattering the throngs of people who were doing the same thing at a more leisurely pace. They stared at the rushing tourists, undoubtedly wondering why they didn't pause to enjoy the mammoth gold chandeliers and magnificent ceilings.

It evolved that the Fabergé eggs were not to be seen. "All special applications must be submitted a month in advance for that exhibit," Rita reported briskly when questioned. But that turned out to be her only omission; they viewed the Italian school of painting on a strict timetable, barely paused at the famous peacock clock in its glass cage, whipped through the corridors for German art, and then were ushered into the Flemish masters without a backward glance. The Spanish, English, and French exhibits were given the same lightning treatment. Fortunately, Rita had a fondness for Rembrandt, so they lingered for ten minutes in his gallery. Immediately a midwestern couple sank onto a wooden bench and slipped their shoes off.

"Poor souls. They've aged ten years in the last hour," Lynda whispered to Ross as they stood in front of Rembrandt's famous work, *Abraham's Sacrifice of Isaac*. She lifted one foot and eased the shoe from her heel. "I know just how they feel. Could we go over to that wall and lean against it while we're waiting?"

He nodded and then frowned as he followed her across the big gallery. "Something wrong with your foot?"

"Make that feet . . . plural," she said grimly. "They're simply suffering from terminal fatigue like the rest of me. Rita must live on brewer's yeast and blackstrap molasses with her borscht. She isn't even breathing hard, and the rest of us look like prison-camp survivors." She gestured toward the weary tourists as they stood numbly in the center of the floor and leaned against pedestals. "They aren't even looking at the pictures anymore," Lynda went on. "I heard one man say he'd pay five dollars for a drink of anything. Even from one of those vending machines where they have community glasses instead of paper cups." When she saw Ross's shoulders start to shake, she added severely, "It isn't funny—that poor old soul sitting on the bench over there has been searching for a ladies' room ever since we were on the second floor one palace back."

"No kidding?" His amused look faded and his mouth settled into stern lines. "Maybe it's time to use a little persuasion on Rita. I doubt if her superiors at Intourist know how zealous she is. I'll have a word with her. Will you be here?"

"Unless they dynamite this wall," she replied, settling her shoulders more firmly against it. "I'm afraid to move. That dragon of a guard in the black dress is giving me the cold and stony."

He glanced over at the guard in question. "That's just her normal expression. Wonder what the hourly wage is here."

"Hardly enough to keep her in carpet slippers. The ones she's wearing have seen better days, too.

Go and talk to Rita. I'm going to close my eyes and think about pitchers of cold lemonade."

She heard his muffled chuckle as she proceeded to do just that. A moment later, however, her curiosity got the better of her, and she glanced across the room to see how he was faring with the energetic Rita.

That young lady was staring up at him with rosy cheeks as he bent attentively over her. Lynda didn't know what he was saying, but it must have been effective, for Rita brought her palms up to her warm face with a gesture of chagrin as she turned to stare at the little old lady on the bench. Then she looked back at Ross and said something which brought forth his engaging smile.

If Lynda had reason to doubt the man's impact on the feminine sex, the capitulation of their Intourist guide offered conclusive proof. In that instant, the girl obviously would have followed him anywhere—even behind the capitalist curtain.

Lynda sighed and shook her head, wondering why newspapers talked about the power of a woman. Put a six-foot, lean, and personable man on display and watch the women start crumbling! She saw him start back toward her and closed her eyes abruptly. It would be just as well if he didn't know what she'd been thinking.

"Everything's all set," he said, pulling up beside her. "Rita's agreed to your taking the little old lady on ahead. One flight up on the stairs at the end of this corridor." He jerked his thumb back toward the Flemish-masters gallery. "She says there's a ladies' room next to the French-impressionist displays. The rest of the tour will meet you in the first gallery on the floor. Okay?"

"Of course. But what about the rest of the women in the group?"

"Rita promised a five-minute rest stop when we get down to the entrance again. Shouldn't be long."

"All right." Lynda craned her head to peer down the room. "End of the corridor and one flight up. I should find that without any trouble." She smiled at him briefly. "See you next to the Monets, if they have any, or the Matisses if they don't."

"Right." He was glancing around. "Better get going now. I'd recommend a strategic withdrawal without any fanfare. Rita was willing to bend a rule or two, but if all the women follow you . . ."

"Say no more. See you upstairs." Lynda walked without hurrying over to the little lady on the bench. She only had to say a few words before the woman jumped up, her tired face ablaze with hope.

Lynda led the way for the two of them, stopping to point out a detail on Rembrandt's canvas of *The Holy Family* before they wandered on out of the gallery. After that, she wasted no time finding the flight of stairs that Rita had mentioned, and a few minutes later, the little lady was all smiles as she dodged behind a wooden door with the cut-out figure of a woman on it.

Lynda watched her disappear and then decided

hat she might as well examine the galleries behind her while she waited to rejoin Ross and the
rest of the group.

That part of the museum was almost empty except for two black-garbed women who served as
guards over the collections. Lynda wandered past
them to admire a group of bronzes on display.
Minutes later, she walked over to some long windows on one side of a gallery and stared down at
the parking area behind the museum. Thank
heaven it wouldn't be long until they could get
back on the bus and return to the ship.

She strolled on to a deserted gallery where the
impressionist exhibition began. Like the rest of
the Hermitage displays, the cards explaining each
work were written only in Russian. Lynda moved
closer to the paintings and tried to decipher the
artists' signatures. The genius of Matisse and Mo-
net needed no translation, and she was so en-
tranced by a row of their offerings that she paid no
attention to some Russian voices beyond the partition masking the next gallery. There was an open
door to the left of her, and she peered around it,
hoping to find more of the French works she ad-
mired.

There was only time to discover that she had
mistakenly wandered into a room where the
guards kept their cleaning supplies when she heard
a muffled movement behind her.

Catching a surprised breath, she'd just started to
whirl around when she saw an arm descend with
sudden force. There was an instant of sharp and

excruciating pain at the side of her neck, even as she opened her lips to scream. Then a wave of darkness swept over her, blotting out everything in its path.

She wasn't conscious to hear the muffled noise her shoes made a moment later as she was dragged still farther into the room. Neither did she hear the door when it was firmly closed behind her, nor the click of the key being turned in the lock. There was another grating of metal when the key was removed, and then only the diminishing tread of careful footsteps.

After that, there was no sound at all.

Chapter Six

The curtain of oblivion was rung down on Lynda with merciful swiftness. The realization that she was missing came painfully slow.

Like a patient who fears his symptoms too much to call a doctor, Ross strolled around the top-floor gallery of impressionist art looking at his watch every two minutes and trying to assure himself that Lynda would certainly come through the archway in the next thirty seconds. The fact that the little woman Lynda had chaperoned was back among them confirmed his feelings of uneasiness. When he noticed Rita shepherding the members of his group toward a down stairway, he decided that something had definitely gone wrong.

"I beg your pardon," he said, elbowing his way to speak to the woman Lynda had rescued. "Could you tell me where Miss Garrett is?" As she stared up at him, clearly uncomprehending, he added brusquely, "The lady who came up to this floor with you . . . a few minutes ago." From the corner of his eye he saw Rita start back toward them, obviously annoyed that they were delaying the others.

"Oh, you mean Lynda! That nice girl who showed me the ladies' . . ." The woman broke off in embarrassment. "I don't know . . . I thought she was here with the rest. Maybe Rita knows. . . ." As the stocky guide came up, the woman said, "Did you see where Lynda went?"

"Lynda?" Rita was obviously at a loss. "Who is this Lynda?"

"Miss Garrett. She came up here with this lady," Ross cut in, wondering which of the damned women was more obtuse—the one who didn't understand plain English or the one who did.

"Ah . . . your friend . . . the pretty lady with the shoes to match her violet dress," Rita responded, showing that feminine observations were the same the world over. "I thought she was with you. Are you sure she's not?"

Ross wanted to say there were a hell of a lot of things he wasn't sure of in the world, but that wasn't one of them. In the interests of further cooperation, he restrained himself. "I haven't seen her," he replied tersely. "Not since she left us downstairs."

Rita pursed her lips. "Nor I. Naturally, I had other things on my mind."

"Naturally."

She disregarded his dry comment and said, "I shall ask the women in charge of the galleries. They would have seen her . . . it is their business."

Ross thought privately that the women guards were more intent on keeping visitors away from the malachite columns and glass showcases than identifying faces, but possibly he was wrong.

When Rita returned, frowning, a few minutes later, it seemed that he wasn't.

"They didn't notice anyone of her description," the guide reported. She turned to the woman who had accompanied Lynda in the first place. "You are certain that she came up to this floor with you?"

"Of course. I wasn't so tired that I could mistake a thing like that." Her head swiveled to Ross for confirmation. "You saw us leave together."

"I know." His expression was grim. "I plan to comb this place inch by inch."

"That will not be allowed," the Intourist guide decided. "Probably your Miss Garrett is waiting for us down at the bus. It is past the time we were to return."

"She wouldn't have left without telling me," Ross declared, but there was an undercurrent of doubt in his voice.

Rita was quick to note it. "We will go down and look. If she is not there, then I must consult my superior."

"For God's sake, how long does that take?" Ross asked, falling into step reluctantly beside her. Visions of Soviet red tape with forms in triplicate obscured his vision as Rita beckoned to the waiting group and they started for the stairs.

"She is downstairs by the main entrance. It will

not be difficult—I can report as soon as we check the bus, if it is necessary. Probably this is much ado about nothing." Rita tossed the phrase off as if she'd been waiting for a chance to use it ever since she'd read Shakespeare. "If we encounter Miss Garrett at the bus, I shall tell her not to stray from the group again, and we shall return to the ship without delay."

"I don't think you'll find her at the bus," Ross muttered doggedly.

Rita stuck out her chin as they started down another flight of stairs. "You are not experienced in these things," she commented, and swept on.

But when they arrived at the parking lot, a look at the bus revealed that it was clearly vacant except for the driver, snoozing in his seat. Rita's mouth tightened, and she used her palm on the door. When the driver jerked awake, she mounted the steps for a hasty conference. A few words and a shake of his head were enough to convey that wherever Lynda had strayed, it wasn't toward tour bus number two.

Rita swept the other members of the group aboard with a peremptory gesture, paying no attention to their mutterings. Lynda's disappearance was proving more interesting than anything else— especially since they were now able to sit down on upholstered bus seats as they discussed it.

If Rita had been inclined to linger, Ross would have turned and made his way back into the museum alone. But the guide was obviously upset that she had allowed one of her sheep to stray, and

Ross was hard put to keep up with her as she hurried back to the palace. He stayed by her side as she searched out a tall blond woman in uniform near the main entrance. Since their conversation was entirely in Russian, he had to wait impatiently while they decided on official policy.

"Ross!" The feminine call made him whirl with sudden hope, which died abruptly as he identified Margareta pushing her way through the crowd. He saw Raoul catch up with her, and together they made their way to his side.

"We saw you out by the bus," Margareta said, breathing hard. "What's going on?"

Raoul cut in. "We were under a tree in the shade waiting for you all to show up. Then suddenly you and"—he jerked his head toward Rita—"our friend there set off as if you were a pair of cross-country runners." He broke off and looked around. "Where's Lynda?"

"I wish to God I knew," Ross exploded. "That's the trouble. We can't find her."

Margareta's eyebrows climbed. "But where did you lose her? And why did you leave her alone?"

Ross was rescued from her barrage when Rita and her superior approached. "We have decided to make a search of the top gallery, Mr. Buchanan," Rita announced. "If your Miss Garrett is not found, then a report must be made at headquarters." She broke off and frowned as she recognized Raoul and Margareta. "You two should be on the bus with the others."

"Nevertheless, we are here," Raoul said just as firmly.

"All this is wasting time," Ross emphasized, starting toward the stairway. "We should have searched that floor fifteen minutes ago."

Raoul touched his elbow warningly. "Easy, my friend. There is no point in causing an incident if it isn't necessary."

"He's right, Ross." Margareta was hurrying up the marble stairs at his side. She cast a glance over her shoulder at the two Intourist guides on their heels. "It's fortunate that the museum is about to close," she went on as they dodged around a group coming down the middle of the stairway. "Most of the visitors will be on their way out by now." When he didn't answer, but merely turned on the landing and started up another flight, she asked, "Are you sure that Lynda didn't go out with another group by mistake? She could be wandering around the grounds, you know."

"There are a half-dozen things she *could* be doing," Ross said irritably as they climbed the final flight. "The fact remains that she promised to meet me in the impressionist gallery. Why in the hell would she change her mind without letting me know?" He was breathing hard after the nonstop climb, but was totally unaware of it.

In this respect, he differed from the others; Rita's plump face was red with exertion, and her coworker was taking the last few steps with decided difficulty.

"How do you want to do it?" Ross asked her when she arrived at the top.

"We will tour the galleries on this floor." Her English was accented but fairly fluent. "That woman"—she nodded toward a guard in black—"will search all the staff sections. We will include the lavatory where your Miss . . ." She looked inquiringly at Rita.

"Garrett," the other mumbled.

"Where your Miss Garrett accompanied the woman from your tour." Her tone showed that that decision was the first glaring mistake in the whole sorry affair.

"I will go with her," Rita muttered, her cheeks still scarlet.

Ross opened his mouth to protest, but Margareta spoke up first. "I'll go too," she told him with a reassuring glance. And in a lower voice, "That way, we'll know for sure."

"Thanks." He watched her follow Rita, who marched toward a roped-off section behind the stairs, beckoning a guard on the way.

"Now we shall take the galleries one by one," the other Intourist guide said to Ross. "Each opens into the next, so the search should be simple. I doubt that we shall find anything." She gestured as they moved into the first big room. "Aside from the benches in the center, you will see there is no place to hide anything. Even the movable walls . . ."

"Partitions," Raoul translated.

She gave him a reproving look, but not as stern

as the one she'd directed toward Rita earlier.
"Even the partitions do not hide anything," she repeated. "Anyone who was ill would be seen by
other visitors."

Their footsteps echoed eerily on the wooden
floors of the big rooms as they went slowly across
them.

"The cleaning crews haven't started yet, have
they?" Ross asked, in the third gallery.

"Not for another hour," she admitted.

Ross moved away from her side to check out a
small window embrasure. "Nothing," he said to
Raoul a minute later when he returned.

By then they had arrived at the next gallery,
close to the end of the impressionist section. The
far wall was bisected by partitions which cloaked a
display of Russian bronzes that Ross had seen earlier. He had given them only a cursory glance, pre-
ferring the paintings of the permanent exhibit.

"We're coming to the end," Raoul murmured.
"Of course, the others may have found something.
There's more of a chance in the staff rooms than
here in the galleries."

"I suppose so." Ross poked his head around the
first partition to inspect two good-sized pieces of
statuary. "Although I can't figure out why Lynda
would go into staff rooms."

"An ordinary visitor wouldn't," the Intourist
guide informed him. "She could have taken ill and
stumbled into one of our cleaner's rooms by mistake," she added grudgingly. "Rita will check."

Ross paused by the second partition. "Are all the staff rooms back by the stairs?"

"I think so." The woman bit her lip in concentration and then shook her head. "No, there is one at this end of the section. It is more convenient for cleaning these galleries. This section was part of the original structure, and in remodeling, the architects tried to limit their changes."

"Yes, I understand." Ross had no desire to hear another lecture. "Perhaps we could look at it . . . as long as we're here."

"Of course." The woman led them past the final partition and moved behind a pillar. "If the room is locked, we shall have to send for a guard with a key. Don't get your hopes up," she said to Ross over her shoulder in a more kindly tone. She reached for the knob on a door designed to blend with the intricate wooden carving mounted on the rest of the wall. "This was moved from another part of the palace. Czarina Catherine the Great commissioned a French woodcarver for the work." Her voice broke off as she stepped on something, and she frowned when she bent down to pick up a key. "I shall speak to the guard. Property of the state must be handled carefully—not thrown about . . ." Her words transcended to a gasp of outrage when Ross couldn't stand it any longer and plucked the key from her fingers. "I will report your interference," she began heatedly, as he put it in the lock.

But when he'd yanked the door open, her anger changed to horrified surprise as he muttered a violent oath and went down on his knees beside a limp figure.

The guide turned to Raoul, her eyes wide. "This is the woman?"

He paused just long enough to nod, and then knelt on the other side of Lynda, who was stirring as Ross raised her to his chest.

"*Ma foi,*" Raoul breathed. "*Pauvre petite!*"

His sympathetic murmurings went unnoticed; all Lynda could comprehend just then was the possessive grasp of strong arms around her and the unmistakable tremor in the deep voice saying her name over and over again. She opened her eyes and focused on Ross's concerned face, inches from hers.

Then she managed the vestige of a smile and struggled to sit upright as he loosened his clasp. A slow survey of her surroundings didn't bring the enlightenment that she'd hoped.

"I . . . I don't understand." Her words were a husky whisper. "What in the dickens are we doing in this place . . . and on the floor," she added, moving her aching hips.

Ross had to clear his throat. "That's what I was hoping you could tell us." At her blank look, he went on gently, "This is a cleaning room in the Hermitage . . . next to the gallery where you were going to wait."

Her eyes widened as reason started to return. "A cleaning room? I remember now . . . I'd just poked my head in here when something hit me."

Her hand went up involuntarily to the side of her neck, which was throbbing painfully.

"Is that where it hurts?" Raoul asked as he bent closer. "The only place?"

"I think so." She used Ross's arm for support, and swayed slightly as she managed to get vertical. "Except for the grandmother of all headaches."

"Maybe you'd better lie down again," Ross suggested, hanging on to her like dear life.

She started to shake her head, and gave it up quickly. "No, just let me have a minute to get back to normal. I'll be all right."

"What is this grandmother of headaches?" the Russian guide was asking Raoul. When he merely shook his head, she was forced to turn to Ross. "Miss Garrett must go down to my office. I shall phone for medical assistance, and an ambulance will take her to the hospital for examination."

"No! I'm not going." Lynda had recovered enough to recall seeing a muddy van with red-cross markings on the street that morning, and she clutched at Ross's arm. "Don't let them take me. Please, Ross . . ."

"Relax, honey." He caught her groping fingers in a warm clasp. "Nobody's going to take you anyplace if you don't want to go."

"I am trying to offer proper medical assistance." The Intourist guide's voice was affronted, with some reason. "There is no need for Miss Garrett to become abusive."

"I'm sure she doesn't mean it that way," Ross

soothed the woman while he kept tight hold of
Lynda. "Just now she isn't feeling well . . ."

"Precisely why I suggest phoning for an ambulance."

Ross felt Lynda stiffen against him, and exerted
a warning pressure. "It's kind of you," he told the
Russian guide, "but I believe that going back to
our ship for a rest might solve everything. If she
doesn't improve there, naturally we will call for
medical help." He heard Lynda mutter "Over my
dead body" and nipped her fingers reprovingly.

"As long as you realize we are not responsible."
The guide continued to lecture them as she led the
way into the gallery. "I shall have to make a written report to my superiors, but for the moment—"

"We'll get Miss Garrett on the bus," Raoul cut
in. He beamed on the Russian woman before turning to Ross. "I believe we can carry Lynda between us."

"That isn't necessary. I can walk to the bus."
Lynda tried to sound as definite as everyone else.

"One thing at a time," Ross cautioned. "Right
now you'll hang on to Raoul on one side and me
on the other. Don't argue."

It was a blow to independent womanhood, but
just then Lynda was relieved to have two autocratic males shoring her up. Her neck felt as if
she'd traded blows with a Japanese wrestler, and
her head throbbed in sympathy. She had a sneak-
ing suspicion that if she'd tried to reach the stairway on her own, it would have been on all fours.

"I will tell Rita that the lost one is found," the

Russian woman informed them at the head of the staircase. "You will go directly to the bus."

"Go directly to jail . . . do not pass Go . . . do not collect two hundred dollars," Lynda murmured, until a pinch from Ross shut her up. "Sorry."

"I should think so." He raised his voice as he affirmed, "Straight to the bus. Naturally we're anxious to get Miss Garrett back to the ship as soon as possible. Will you tell Miss Sundstrom? The fair-haired lady with Rita."

"Ah . . . *that* one." The guard nodded. "She will accompany Rita and meet you on the bus as well."

"Thank you."

They parted amicably, with relief on their part and some lingering suspicion on hers as she watched them go down the first flight of steps.

"What was all that about not collecting two hundred dollars?" Raoul wanted to know as they reached the first landing.

"A bad joke," Ross told him, "but thank God, it shows that Lynda's head is still attached and functioning."

"I'll let you know when I'm able to wriggle my ears again," Lynda said. "Would you mind not talking about me as if I'd been reported missing?"

"When we get some privacy, I sure as hell plan to learn why you were missing in the first place."

"There's no need to take her head off again, Ross," Raoul remonstrated. "Probably Lynda has a logical explanation for all this."

Ross stopped at the bottom of the stair landing to let her rest for a moment. "I wonder." He gazed down at her intently. "Do you?"

"No." She didn't look up, and he had to bend his head to hear the fierce monosyllable.

Ross frowned, as she didn't elaborate. "Maybe I should have let that woman call a doctor for you, after all."

Her glance did come up then to meet his. "If you had, I'd never have forgiven you," she said flatly. "I don't want to talk about it—I don't even want to think about it."

"Lynda, *mon ānge,* he isn't serious. Don't look like that. We won't let anyone take you away from us. Isn't that right, Ross?" Raoul insisted.

Ross started to reply, and then closed his mouth again. When he finally spoke, he was obviously choosing his words with care. "That's up to Lynda."

She spoke lightly, trying to ignore his stormy features. "Right now . . . I'll settle for a safe passage back to the ship."

"Agreed." He tightened his grip on her elbow. "I'll go along with that. At any rate . . . for now."

Chapter Seven

After dinner that evening Ross was convinced he should have taken a firmer stand.

Not that there was anything he could do about it by then. He and Lynda were back on the sightseeing bus en route to an evening at the ballet under Rita's determined supervision.

As they retraced their route to the center of town in the early evening, the streets were even more deserted than before, and the bus passengers were talking happily to their companions rather than looking out the windows.

Lynda proved the exception to the rule, keeping her attention determinedly on the deserted sidewalks and shops, so that Ross was given a frustrating view of the back of her head. He knew she was doing it deliberately; the atmosphere had been charged between them ever since he had seen her to her stateroom that afternoon after the Hermitage fiasco and tried to get a straight story about what had happened.

Lynda had been reluctant to discuss it. She stubbornly declared that all she remembered was hear-

ing fragments of a conversation in Russian before
she was felled.

"But that conversation you overheard . . . was it
two men, or women, or what?" Ross had perse-
vered, trying to ignore her drawn face as she rested
on her berth. "You must remember something."

"I don't." Lynda's response wasn't encouraging.
Aspirin hadn't done much to ease the pain of the
little men who were tromping over her head in
hobnailed boots just like in the television commer-
cials. As much as she appreciated Ross's concern,
just then all she wanted to do was close her eyes
and give thanks that she was safely back in her
stateroom on the Finnish ship.

Her unhappiness didn't go unnoticed by Ross,
but he had stayed stubbornly by her porthole a little longer. Long enough to say, "At least you're
certainly not going to that ballet tonight."

Being a bachelor, he didn't realize that issuing
an ultimatum was the worst possible way to con-
front a member of the feminine sex. Lynda, who,
until that moment, had been thinking the same
thing, abruptly changed her mind.

"I most certainly am going," she answered,
pushing up on an elbow to add emphasis to her
words. "You don't expect me to stay here in bed
on the one night we're in Russia! This is my only
chance."

Ross would have liked to verbally consign the
entire Russian ballet company to the fiery depths,
but he recovered in time to avoid saying so. Instead he tried a new tactic. "Lynda, be reasonable.

You've had a terrible afternoon. Anybody with any sense . . ." He choked that off when he saw her stormy expression, and started again. "Look, you don't want to make yourself really sick. The first thing you have to remember when you're traveling in foreign countries is to take care of yourself and not overdo. A good night's sleep, and you'll probably come out of this without any harm." His voice coaxed her. "Now, what do you say?"

"I'm going to the ballet."

"Oh, for God's sake . . ."

Her eyes flashed with anger. "I didn't say that *you* had to go to the ballet. Why don't you get a good night's sleep? You need it more than I do, if you're going to keep losing your temper every five minutes."

"Whenever I'm around you, I lose it a damned sight faster than that." He stomped toward the door. "I'm certainly not going to stay here and argue with you."

She waited until he was halfway through the cabin door before she broke down and asked, "*Are* you coming to the ballet?"

"Probably," he growled over his shoulder. "It isn't safe to let you out alone, and you're still my responsibility."

He said nothing about another fact that he'd discovered only a few hours before—that he felt strangely uncomfortable whenever she was out of his sight. Just then it didn't lessen his urge to whale the daylights out of her. It was either that or make violent love to her, and his reasoning wasn't so far gone as to try the latter course.

Unfortunately, Lynda had no idea of what he was thinking. She could only see his angry face and hear the hateful phrase "you're my responsibility" lingering in the air between them. That caused a pain in the region of her heart which was far worse than any of her other ailments.

"I'll probably see you on the bus," she told him in as distant a way as she could.

"What about your dinner?"

She raised her eyebrows disdainfully.

"You have to eat," he persisted from his place in the doorway.

"That is *not* your responsibility. That's between me and the stewardess." She punched up her pillow and leaned back. "Would you please close the door behind you when you go out."

The thud with which he closed it loosened the hinges appreciably.

Ross was still irritable when he met her at the bottom of the gangway and they set out for the evening performance. Secretly he was relieved to see that she looked much better. Her black sheer wool dress with its white satin ascot emphasized the translucent quality of her complexion and effectively hid the bruise on the side of her neck. She was holding her head high when she received her shore pass from the Russian guard and turned to greet Ross.

"You needn't have bothered," she told him. "I feel fine, thanks. So if you want to do something else, it's perfectly all right." She was silenced when he took her arm in a grasp that showed she could skip any further platitudes.

They marched on down the dock in a starched silence. Lynda was distracted by the figure of the Russian guard standing at stiff attention when they walked by the bow of the ship. "How long has he been like that, for heaven's sake?" she asked in a low voice as they passed. "It can't be the same soldier we saw this morning. . . ."

"I hope not. Otherwise they'd have the makings of another revolution on their hands."

She nodded and looked over her shoulder. "Aren't Raoul and Margareta coming with us?"

"Nope. They decided on the circus and left a half-hour ago. If we're back aboard at the same time, they want us to join them for a drink." He shot her a wary glance. "If you feel like it, of course."

Ross sounded considerably more subdued than he had before, and Lynda decided that she could be equally gracious. "Thanks. Let's wait and see, shall we?" Then she frowned as she murmured, "I wonder why they chose the circus."

The answer wasn't long in coming. Their bus driver had no sooner left the parking lot than Rita began apologizing for the forthcoming ballet. "It is to be regretted," she said pontifically, "that the season for our famous Kirov Ballet is over. However, we shall see some of their gifted beginners in a special recital tonight." She paused as a groan of disappointment rose from the tour group. Lynda could feel Ross stir restlessly on the seat beside her and didn't dare meet his glance. He had been reluctant to see good ballet; now he was faced with a makeshift "special" performance. She bit her lip and turned to stare out the window before he could say "I told you so."

The only person who appeared enchanted by the prospect ahead was their Intourist guide. As the bus moved speedily through the quiet streets, she gave a lengthy recital of her own, explaining how ballet stars were trained in the Soviet Union, and extolling the wonders of the Kirov. Her larded description of the budding ballerinas on the evening's program was mercifully cut short by the arrival of the bus in front of a dingy theater.

"Cheer up," Ross whispered to Lynda as they got out of their seats and followed the others to the door, "it might be better than we think."

But even his determined air of optimism began to fade when Rita announced that they would have to wait in the theater lobby because the bus was early. There were no chairs in the foyer, and the refreshment stand tucked in the corner accepted only Russian money. A hastily called conference of the visitors proved that there wasn't a ruble or kopek in anybody's wallet, with the possible exception of Rita's. And *she* was at a prudent distance, talking to a woman in a black dress who was in charge of the cloakroom.

"I've never seen less likelihood of making a touch," Ross reported after a quick look at them. "I hope you weren't thirsty," he added to Lynda.

She shook her head and then searched her purse for a handkerchief. "Just hot," she said, blotting her cheeks. "Does it seem warm in here to you?"

"Lord, yes! They must have somebody stoking the boiler. I wish I had nerve enough to take off my coat, but that dragon in the black dress would tell me to put it back on again."

Lynda gave a gurgle of laughter. "She's big enough to insist."

"Probably throws the discus every four years." He leaned against the wall behind them. "Oh, well, maybe it'll be cooler when we get in the auditorium."

"I hope you're right." She rested against the wall beside him, happy to accept the more relaxed atmosphere between them. At least Ross wasn't a man who sulked when everything didn't go right. This was fortunate, because there were more surprises in store—all of them bad.

When a buzzer sounded twenty minutes later, the usher drew back the curtains and allowed them to file into the small theater. Ross took one look at the armless wooden seats and groaned. "Not an upholstered cushion in the place."

The bare bulbs in an iron chandelier over their heads cast a brilliant light on other inadequacies—the empty orchestra pit, the faded blue velour stage curtain, and, at one side, the worn wooden steps leading up to it.

Ross ushered Lynda into a row of seats halfway down the room and sat down himself, trying to fit his knees around the wooden chair in front of him.

"I can move over and give you more room," Lynda said hastily. "A midget must have designed this."

"The same one who designs economy-class seats for airplane companies," he growled, shifting his length diagonally in the space she vacated. "Do you still have enough room?"

Lynda felt the warmth of his thigh against hers and took an unsteady breath. "Fine, thanks. Shouldn't the musicians be warming up?"

"I'm not sure there are any. If we had a program, we could find out. Provided, of course, we could read Russian . . . which we can't."

"Well, at least there'll be an announcement. Then we'll know what's going on."

"It shouldn't be long now," he confirmed, looking back. "That same woman has drawn the curtains at the back. Next they'll dim the lights. . . ."

The chandelier overhead obliged on cue, with one small difference.

Lynda drew in her breath sharply as stygian darkness settled over the stunned audience. "They turned them off completely. I can't see a thing."

Ross fumbled for her hand and captured it in a reassuring grip. "More dramatic this way. Ah—now we're in business." That came when a blue spotlight darted uncertainly about on the curtain and then homed in on a tuxedo-clad MC who appeared from the wings, struggling with a heavy floor microphone.

His first words showed that their hosts had decided not to bother with foreign translations for the night. Their commentary was to be exclusively in Russian. As far as the audience was concerned it might as well have been in ancient Sanskrit.

After the initial shock, the visitors sat in polite rows waiting for the commentary to end. The chatty MC beamed on them and finally waved for the curtains to part. A bare stage showed why they hadn't heard any musicians tuning up. Instead, there was the amplified sound of a phonograph needle sliding across a record and being brought back to the proper niche. Then the music of "Darktown Strutters' Ball" blared forth, and a brilliantly attired quartet of dancers leaped into an exhibition of modern dance.

Ross's face didn't move a muscle, but after five minutes of violent choreography, Lynda could feel his shoulders start to shake with helpless amusement. She gave him a warning jab with her elbow and waited until the end of the number to say, under cover of polite applause, "If you say 'I told you so' . . . I swear I'll push you off the gangplank when we get back to the ship. Who would have dreamed that ballet in Leningrad would be like this!"

"Actually, they're not bad . . . considering the handicaps. That stage floor must have been built by Peter the Great."

"I know. It's like an off-Broadway theater where they haven't paid the rent. And I didn't want to see the Charleston or apache dancing—I wanted to see classical ballet. If you dare mention dancing bears in the circus, I'll . . ."

". . . toss me overboard when we get back to the ship," he repeated. His clasp on her fingers tightened reassuringly. "I understand the bears don't dance either—they ice-skate. But things may get better here."

She took a deep breath as the master of ceremonies reappeared, dragging his microphone behind him. "There's only one way for it to go."

Later that night, on the way back to the ship, she had to admit that the evening had a robust charm. The dancers had worked hard, and the audience, after overcoming its initial disappointment, had applauded their determination and sheer exuberance.

"After all," Ross said as the bus speeded through the deserted thoroughfares, "you can watch Russian ballet in New York this winter. That's probably why they're not performing in Leningrad they're resting for the tour." He watched her lips curve in response and asked, "How are you feeling?" When she hesitated, he went on brusquely, "This time, you can tell the truth."

"Not bad, really. All things considered."

"Ummm." His monosyllable was frankly doubting, and he put a firm arm across her shoulders and pulled her close against him. "That means you're hurting like hell. I won't say 'I told you so,'" he added, "but you'd better take advantage of my shoulder until we get back to the ship."

Lynda didn't bother to hide her relief. "I ran out of steam around the second act. Sure you don't mind?"

"Don't be a damned fool." The reply was terse and eminently satisfying.

There were a few moments of silence—this time a comfortable one between them. Then Lynda stirred and said softly, "Ross, will you see Margareta tonight after we get back to the ship?"

"I suppose so. Why?"

"If you have a chance . . . ask her if she saw Birger today."

"Are you still thinking of that?" His tone was amused. "You're not trying to make something sinister out of it?"

"Not really . . . but I'm curious. Besides," she wheedled, "you know her well enough to ask embarrassing questions, and I don't."

"Plus the fact that you're going straight to bed once you get back to the ship." He felt her body stiffen and then relax once again.

"All right," she capitulated with a smothered laugh. "Right now the idea of bed seems heavenly."

"I should think so. You'll notice that I'm being a gentleman and ignoring your provocative remark."

"That's only because you know I'm too darned tired to fight back right now." She heard his stifled laugh and raised her head. "Don't get the wrong idea about that," she added severely.

"Wouldn't think of it," he said, pushing her head back down. "All right, I'll hang around the bar and try to pump Margareta or Raoul discreetly."

"Why Raoul? He isn't a particular friend of Birger's, is he?"

"Not that I've heard." Ross frowned and stared out the bus window. "I'm more curious about why Timo Mäki was visiting in a Russian military center. The man's been outspoken in his support of the Western powers. Too much so for some government officials in Scandinavia who try to keep the waters smooth. Raoul would know more about it; he's traveling around on the Continent most of the time."

"I wonder . . ." she began, and then broke off. "No, that's silly," she concluded. "I'm imagining things!"

"You're also going to get another lump if you don't finish your sentences. What in the devil are you talking about?"

She was glad that the dark interior of the bus hid the warm color of her cheeks. "It was nothing. For a second I wondered if there could be any connection between their appearance in Leningrad and the fact that I was stuffed in a broom closet."

"I don't see how," Ross said, after considering it. "There isn't a chance in a hundred that Timo looked up to identify you, and you said Birger Lindh's attention was on Mäki. Isn't that right?" As she nodded slowly, he said, "It's more likely you interrupted some black-market transaction in the museum gallery, and the participants didn't want to chance identification."

"In my fluent Russian?"

He chuckled. "Yes, but they didn't know that. You were just a stranger."

"I suppose you're right." She sat up with a sigh as the bus driver turned into the brightly lit port area with its high fence. "At least it makes more sense than anything I've been able to come up with."

"The best thing you can do is to forget it. When we get to the ship, take a couple aspirin and get in bed with a nice hot-water bottle. By tomorrow morning you'll feel like a new woman." He saw her eyebrows climb in mild derision. "No charge for office calls. Twenty-four-hour service, and an excellent bedside manner . . . so I'm told."

Lynda knew better than to pursue that. She gathered her purse and pulled her wrap around her shoulders as the bus pulled up with a squeal of brakes in front of the customs building. "I'll remember. Thanks for the use of your shoulder. I appreciated it."

His expression sobered, and he put a detaining hand on her arm as the other passengers started shuffling into the aisle. "Then can I request a favor of you?" He saw her questioning glance and smiled reassuringly. "I'm not about to ask you to work your passage . . . so relax. I just want you to stick close to me tomorrow. There isn't a chance in a thousand that you'll have any more trouble, but Peterhof Palace is a big place."

"You don't have to convince me," she said. "I don't like odds of even a thousand to one when I'm this far from home."

An expression of relief came over his features. "Then how about 'going steady' for the rest of the time we're here?"

"I'd love to," she said fervently.

"Good! We'll start now," he said, getting up and preceding her down the aisle. "And don't you forget about it tomorrow."

Ross needn't have worried about the possibility of Lynda changing her mind. The next morning, when her travel alarm sounded, it took only a glance through the porthole toward the Russian guards on the dock to remind her of the frightening episode at the Hermitage. Even if their official uniforms hadn't triggered her memory, her stiff muscles would have provided instant recall. She pulled down the porthole blind and turned thankfully away to get dressed.

Ross caught up with her just outside the dining salon and followed her to the breakfast buffet line. "You don't look as if you suffered any ill effects," he said lightly. Privately he thought that she still seemed pale from her ordeal, but it was obvious by her carefully applied makeup that she was determined to ignore it. Even her coral linen dress looked bright and cheerful.

"You're a dreadful liar, but I appreciate the thought," Lynda told him as she selected a tray and moved toward the display of fruit. After she'd helped herself, she lingered while he made his selection, and noticed finely drawn lines around his eyes and mouth that weren't there the day before.

His outfit of gray slacks and sport shirt under a navy-blue suede jacket couldn't be faulted, but he had an air of tenseness which didn't go with the casual garb.

"What's the matter?" He'd glanced up and intercepted her searching appraisal before she could look away. "Did I miss a spot when I shaved?" He tested his chin with inquisitive fingers.

"Don't be silly. You look very nice." She slid her tray on toward the bowl of boiled eggs.

"I'd look better if I'd had four more hours' sleep. Margareta and Raoul never want to go to bed. The things I do for you, my girl." He caught up with her as she stared at the eggs. "Now what?"

"I was wondering if the ones in the middle were warmer. Don't Finns ever eat scrambled eggs or fried ones?"

Ross poked down for a warm egg, too. "When in Helsinki . . ."

". . . don't expect bacon and coddled eggs for breakfast," she finished. "I know. At least their coffee's good. Shall I get you a cup?"

"Okay. I'll find some bread and butter and stake out a table for us."

"Will Margareta and Raoul be down for breakfast?"

"I doubt it. Both of them are staying in town today."

Lynda was still thinking about that when she joined him at a table against the wall a few minutes later. "Don't they want to see Peterhof?" she asked.

Ross didn't have any trouble understanding her mental shorthand. "Not enough to go out on a tour bus. Margareta said that she intended to shop in the Beriozhka, and Raoul plans to sleep most of the forenoon. It was late when they got in from the circus."

Lynda was trying, unsuccessfully, to take the top off her egg. She glanced over at a Swedish woman at the next table, who had achieved it by a gentle tapping with the back of her spoon. "When I do that," Lynda said, "I get pieces of shell through the whole darned egg."

Ross managed to remove the top of his without any trouble. "I'm beginning to understand your preoccupation with scrambled eggs. Want some help?"

"If that three-year-old can manage," Lynda said grimly, nodding toward a toddler sitting nearby, "I should be able to."

Ross watched her with amusement and said finally, "Never mind—they'll serve them again tomorrow morning, and you'll do better then. Have some bread. . . ." He passed her a plate. "I wonder if toasters went out with the Middle Ages?"

Lynda started to laugh. "We're a fine pair. The trouble is that we're creatures of habit. A change is probably good for us."

"No doubt." He looked sheepish. "I told you I needed more sleep. Now you know for sure."

"I think you're remarkable in your forbearance," she replied solemnly. "The way you're carefully not mentioning the circus performance last night. You needn't be so tactful. A woman I met in the companionway said that it was simply marvelous. And when I think of how I insisted on the ballet . . ." She shook her head.

"It wasn't so bad," he said, trying to sound as if he meant it. When she began to laugh, his own lips curved. "All right, it was god-awful, but we didn't know the regular season was over. At least, with Peterhof today, we're on safe ground."

"You've seen it before?"

"Yes, and it's well worth another trip. Actually, we travel the road the Nazis used when they advanced on Leningrad during World War II."

"Tell me more." She wrinkled her nose at him across the table. "I'd rather listen to you than Rita."

"Flattery—thy name is woman," he reproved, but leaned back in his chair and went on. "You'll see the monument which marks the outer defense line of the city during the siege. Then it's just a short drive to the Summer Palace. It was named Peterhof in honor of Peter the Great, who decided to build his own Versailles there in 1711. Later on, Catherine II and subsequent czars added a few little finishing touches." Ross's eyes gleamed with sudden laughter. "Though 'little' is hardly the word for anything that involves three hundred acres of gardens and a hundred and twenty-nine fountains. The fountains lead out to a marine canal which eventually flows into the Gulf of Finland."

Lynda put her elbows on the table, intent on his words. "It sounds absolutely fabulous."

"It is. And the hometown folks would be the first to agree with you. Margareta says there are always busloads of Russians who come to enjoy their heritage from the czars. I hope you feel up to battling the crowds."

"Don't worry. I feel fine. But even if I didn't, you'd have a hard time keeping me off the bus." Her sudden smile was heartfelt. "This is a wonderful place to visit. I haven't thanked you properly for giving me the chance to come."

Her enthusiasm made Ross pause. "How can you say that after what happened yesterday? I was planning to send you an armful of roses by way of apology when we got back to Helsinki."

"In that case, I wouldn't think of changing your mind." She folded her napkin and put it on the table. "We can talk about it later, though. Right now, I'll go get my things."

"Good idea." He checked his watch. "There's no harm in being early for the bus."

The sun came out of hiding by the time they left the environs of the city, shining peacefully onto the flat green countryside. Once the crowded apartment-lined blocks were left behind, they could see the new construction projects going up in the suburbs. There were the usual lines of people waiting for buses and interurban tram cars, making Lynda think that Russian citizens must be the most patient in the world; certainly they had more experience standing in line than any others.

A few more miles, and the suburban construction gave way to small homes with modest vegetable-garden plots around them. Groups of men and women were out working the fields, the former stripped to the waist in the gentle spring sunshine.

They weren't the only ones enjoying the unusually warm weather; the passengers on the bus were chatting happily after spending the previous day together. As the bus neared Peterhof, Rita brought out her notebook and repeated the statistics that Ross had related to Lynda over the breakfast table. But even repetition couldn't dull the awe-inspiring sight of the gilded domes when they first appeared ahead of them.

For the next few hours Lynda stayed happily beside Ross as they toured through high-ceilinged palace rooms which showed the grandeur and opulence of former days. Afterward they strolled through the acres of fountains, which had been repaired after the damages of Nazi occupation. Each one was faithfully restored to its eighteenth-century design.

Lynda was weary when they finally got on the bus for the trip back to town, but felt her strength returning when their guide announced that they would be shopping at the Beriozhka tourist shops before finally returning to the ship.

Some forty minutes later, they pulled up in front of a small section of shops, where the parking lot was crowded with Intourist buses. Ross grinned as he saw the sparkle in Lynda's eyes.

"You're coming, too . . . aren't you?" she asked, checking her supply of traveler's checks as they waited for a chance to get down the aisle. "I need some expert advice."

"It depends whether your taste runs to wooden toys, lacquer boxes, or caviar. They're the best buys."

"Maybe a few of each." She peered up at him hopefully. "If I can afford it."

"That's no problem. The government's priced everything at about fifty percent of the value in these shops."

"You shouldn't have told me," she said over her shoulder as they moved down the bus aisle. "No woman can resist a bargain like that. It's a good thing I've already paid for my plane ticket home."

He shook his head. "You sound like a hopeless case."

"Not really. I'd just like to be." She jumped down to the pavement. "Lead on. Toys first, I think . . . for my nephews, then a lacquer box for my mother."

Ross grinned and turned her toward the first door. "Then caviar . . . for me."

It took only a few minutes for Lynda to discover that the Beriozhka was a Russian version of the traditional bargain basement. There were wire shopping carts available, and the shoppers had most of them piled high with goodies in no time at all. Checkout stands were manned by multilingual Soviet clerks with computers and cash registers at their fingertips. They managed the most complex currency conversions in seconds and appeared supremely bored by the whole affair. The customers, by contrast, were beaming over their purchases and pulling them out of their wrappings to admire them all over again even as they left the checkout stands.

Lynda's purchases included a wooden bear with movable arms, two lacquer boxes, and a bone chess set she hadn't been able to resist when Ross finally urged her down to a section with piled displays of caviar and champagne. Clusters of tourists were excitedly discussing the prices in German, French, Danish, and two or three other languages that Lynda couldn't identify. She and Ross waited patiently for the shoppers in front of them to make their choice at a towering display before they moved up to concentrate on the glass jars of Russian caviar. Lynda picked up one of the containers and started to ask Ross if he thought it would be safe in her suitcase en route home, when a female voice nearby said angrily, "There's no use going on about all this. I didn't ask you to come to Leningrad—I didn't even want you here. All you've done is make everything more difficult."

It took Lynda only an instant to recognize the hidden voice as Margareta's. She raised inquiring eyebrows at Ross. He put a warning finger to his lips as a man's tones came through the piled cartons of champagne separating the shop aisles.

"Don't talk to me that way! Not after the trouble you've gotten into," he was accusing Margareta. "You were the one who should have stayed away. There was no real reason for you to be here this weekend. Unless Timo has changed and wants you in attendance seven days a week." There was a harsh laugh. "I hope he pays you well for such devotion to duty."

Lynda's eyes widened. "Birger?" Her lips shaped the name soundlessly, and Ross nodded. Evidently he was feeling guilty at their eavesdropping, because he picked up two small containers of caviar and jerked his head toward the checkstand.

Lynda nodded and started to follow, when the next exchange made Ross pause, and she almost bumped into him.

"I'm sick of hearing about Timo . . . Timo . . . Timo," Margareta said furiously. "He's the only person you can think of, and you're a fool to waste your time being jealous. Ross Buchanan and the girl Lynda are the ones you should be concentrating on."

"Lynda! Don't be ridiculous!" Birger dismissed the idea. "She knows nothing. The girl is on a simple buying trip. You might be right about Buchanan, but there's no proof. That's not the point," Birger went on. "Once the drawings are delivered in the next day or so, your part in this will be finished. Then there will be no more arguments and no more trips. You will do as I say for a change."

"Dearest, be reasonable," Margareta pleaded, her voice more tender than either Lynda or Ross had ever heard it. "It's for both our sakes that I came on this trip."

"Not for mine. Timo might be suspicious of the

Americans, but he's the only one. Ross Buchanan arrived too late to be any threat to the project, and Lynda is merely an attractive compatriot of his. Bedroom politics are the only game he's playing with her." Birger sounded amused.

Margareta wasn't, and clearly didn't believe him. "If she's merely a passing affair, why did the two of them show such interest in Saari's death?"

"That newspaper story was just bad luck."

"Luck! It was foolish to take such a risk with the man." Margareta was autocratic in her pronouncement. "And just last night, Ross was probing to know if I had seen you here."

"What did you tell him?"

"Nothing, of course. Give me credit for that." Her voice dropped, as she evidently consulted her watch. "And we shouldn't be here together now. It's getting close to sailing time."

Ross didn't wait for any more. Catching Lynda by the hand, he dragged her hastily away from the display and toward a checkout line at the far end of the big room. Fortunately, at that moment an extra cashier was pressed into service nearby. Ross said, "Come on . . . over here," and Lynda found herself at the head of a new line beside him, out-flanking a Polish man carrying a balalaika and two Matrushka dolls.

As the cashier was figuring out the amount of their purchase, Lynda said reprovingly to Ross, "That fellow with the balalaika looks like he plans to hit you over the head with it."

"Don't joke about it," Ross muttered as he

handed the cashier some money for the caviar and picked up the jars. "Can you stuff these in your shopping bag?"

"Yes, of course." She packed them carefully alongside the wooden bear, and stood back as Ross tucked the whole package under his arm. "Do I dare look over my shoulder?"

"Not until we're outside the store," he commanded. "Fortunately, our bus is parked close to the entrance. Maybe we can get in without being seen."

Lynda strolled among the other tourists toward the door, stopping for an instant to admire a display of wooden peasant dolls near the entrance. Once through the doors, she and Ross moved quickly to the curb, where their bus waited. Unfortunately, the driver was engaged in adjusting his rear-vision mirror, and they had to wait for him to open the door.

"Damn!" Ross ground out as they cooled their heels on the pavement.

"It's pretty hard to fade out of sight, so we might as well look around," Lynda said. "Otherwise, Margareta and Birger *will* be suspicious."

"Mmmm." Ross didn't sound too sure, but he was curious himself to see if their withdrawal had gone undetected. His casual glance toward the end of the parking lot showed that it hadn't been a tremendous success. Both Margareta and Birger were standing by the side of a small car, staring back at him. For an instant Ross debated whether to recognize them. Then he managed what he hoped was a surprised smile and waved. Carrying the charade further, he turned to Lynda. "Guess who's watching us by the driveway to the street? Look surprised, for God's sake!"

But when they turned back again, the other couple had gotten in the car, and Birger was already cramping the steering wheel for a sharp turn out onto the arterial which led back to the port area.

Chapter Eight

It was fully a quarter of an hour later before Rita was able to round up all of her straggling brood and the bus could set off for the ship.

Lynda and Ross spent the time mildly disagreeing about the conversation they had overhead. There was one point, however, on which they were both in complete accord: Margareta's presence on the Leningrad cruise wasn't the blithe holiday outing they'd thought.

Ross was even more explicit. "The sooner we all part company, the easier I'll feel. It's good there's only one more night before we can get away from this rotten cloak-and-dagger stuff."

"I suppose you're right," Lynda said, wondering if she were expected to retreat with him or go off on her own.

"Damn it, I *know* I'm right." The couple across the bus aisle looked over in surprise at his outburst, and he lowered his voice. "For some reason, we've gotten tangled in a shady mess of Timo and Birger's making. I don't exactly understand how they figure in it, but I don't like the sound of things. From what the newspapers said about Saari, somebody plays rough in their league."

"I'm not disputing that," Lynda told him. "I just wonder what drawings Birger was talking about."

"It's hard to tell." Ross frowned as he tried to concentrate. "Could it be some new project at Arusha that Birger's designed? No, that would be a tempest in a teapot." He winced at his choice of words before saying, "Sorry, I didn't mean that," and started over again. "Maybe he's doing some free-lance stuff that pays better."

"And is strictly illegal." She bit her lip. "Could be. If Mr. Saari was involved somehow."

Ross nodded. "I think we're getting warmer. At least, your curiosity about Saari had spectacular results. Margareta immediately tabbed us as prime suspects."

"Birger wasn't impressed," Lynda said, trying to sound casual as she remembered the man's pithy comment about her connection with Ross.

Ross chose to ignore that. He kept his glance riveted on the seat ahead of them as he said thoughtfully, "I wonder exactly what Saari did to end up thirty feet under the Bay of Finland."

Lynda shuddered. "As long as you're asking for answers, you'd better put Timo Mäki's name on the list. When we saw him yesterday, he didn't look like a businessman playing weekend games with his blond secretary."

"Unless he planned to meet her later in the day."

Lynda considered it and then shook her head. She kept her voice low as she replied. "They wouldn't pick Leningrad for that—not with all the rest of the hotel rooms in Europe. For one thing, I understand the rates here are absolutely exorbitant."

Ross gave a surprised snort of laughter. "Now I know what it takes to impress you."

She responded to his teasing good-naturedly. "I appreciate the thought, but don't bother. This isn't the town for a weekend of sin. As a matter of fact, Helsinki is going to look marvelous when we sail back in the harbor."

"Well, you can take a quick look at it, but keep your bags packed. Raoul and I will see you safely out of danger as soon as we can make some reservations. How does Copenhagen sound for your next stop? The Danes never let intrigue interfere with business, and I can recommend the beer."

Lynda clutched her parcel as their bus took a corner without slackening speed. "You forget, I have a job to do in Helsinki. I can't just pick up and leave because I've collected some goose bumps. Once Margareta and Birger know that they have nothing to fear from us—"

"Wait a minute," Ross cut in authoritatively. "You're certainly not going to have any discussions with them about this. At the moment, they don't know what we overheard—if anything."

"Exactly." Lynda knew she was being stubborn, but Ross was just as guilty; he couldn't brusquely issue a set of orders like a field commander and

expect her to obey them without question. "Why
on earth should I take to my heels over a lot of
unfounded suspicions? We don't have one iota of
proof."

"I should think you'd be the last one to split
hairs over that."

"What do you mean?"

"Have you forgotten what happened to you in
the Hermitage yesterday? You weren't in very
good shape when we found you, and I don't think
you should stick around trying for a matched pair
of concussions," he added brutally.

After that, the ride back to the pier continued
without any more conversation. Ross's expression
was stern, indicating that he had made up his
mind for both of them and didn't intend to change
it. Lynda gave him a quick glance now and then
from the corner of her eye but kept her own features noncommittal. Inwardly, her thoughts were
chaotic as she considered his words. It made sense to
leave Helsinki rather than be drawn unwittingly
into more trouble. On the other hand, Ross's casual invitation to visit Copenhagen could be more
dangerous still. There was no reason to expect him
to carry on a platonic friendship with her all over
Scandinavia. Still less to hope that he wouldn't
misconstrue her motives if she accepted his next
invitation. Yet she couldn't come right out and ask
if a passing affair was what he had in mind.

Raoul's sudden appearance at the doorway of
the customs building when they got off the bus
helped bridge the awkward silence.

"I see you're making sure that you don't miss the sailing either," Ross told him heartily, his voice sounding false to his own ears as he stood stiffly by Lynda's side. It was the first time he could remember when he wanted to turn a woman over his knee and beat her for being so obstinate. He shoved his hands in his trouser pockets to lessen the temptation. Then, encountering Raoul's puzzled look, he came back to the present. "I beg your pardon . . . what did you say?"

"I've just had some news that makes it necessary to change my plans," Raoul repeated. "That's why I was here. The customs house is the only place I could use the telephone." His expression was anxious as he faced Ross. "Would it inconvenience you if I caught an early plane out of Helsinki tomorrow for Paris? Trying for reservations here is next to impossible," he went on with disgust. "If I can put things right in Paris, I'll rejoin you in Copenhagen shortly. It would only mean delaying your itinerary for a day or two there."

"Don't worry about it. My timing's not that vital." Ross put a firm hand under Lynda's elbow, even as the three of them walked into the customs building and through the door leading to the pier. "I hope you won't have any trouble settling your difficulties in Paris."

Raoul grimaced and lifted his hands in an expressive gesture. "An elderly aunt. She is supposed to have surgery and now has decided against it. No one can change her mind except . . ." He hesitated delicately.

Lynda smiled and filled in the missing words. "Except that you're a favorite of hers, and possibly she might listen to you."

"So my mother thinks." His words deprecated the idea. "It is the least I can do. So if Ross doesn't mind . . ."

"And he doesn't," confirmed that individual. "I'll meet you in Copenhagen. It's just as well. I was thinking of changing my own plans." He kept his glance studiously away from Lynda's.

"Then it's all settled." Raoul beamed on them both. "I see you spent some money at the Beriozhka," he teased Lynda. "Did you exhaust all of your bank account?"

"There's a horrible dent in it," she acknowledged, "but I don't mind. Even Ross couldn't resist the caviar."

"Let's hope that it doesn't leak over the shirts in my suitcase before I get home." Ross was scanning the passengers walking down the pier ahead of them, and the group filing up the gangway after retrieving their passports from the Russian guard. "Has Margareta come back on board yet?"

Raoul nodded. "About ten minutes ago, I think. I was telephoning at the time, and I just caught a glimpse of her when she went by."

"Was she alone?" Lynda kept her voice studiously casual.

"I don't really know. There were a lot of passengers coming in the building then, because one of the buses was unloading. Why? Is something wrong?"

"No, of course not. I just wondered." So much for her attempt to keep things low-key, Lynda thought wryly. He had nosed out her intentions like a prize-winning pointer.

"I'm surprised you didn't see her at the Beriozhka," Raoul persisted. "She usually shops there when she's in Leningrad. The prices are much less here than the same article with duty added to it in Helsinki."

"Probably we just missed in our timing," Ross put in mildly. "I thought I saw her leaving the parking lot when we were getting on the bus. Isn't that right, Lynda?" His glance dared her to dispute it, even as his grip on her elbow tightened in warning.

There was a perceptible pause. Then Lynda made a vague murmur of assent and tried to pretend that her only interest was in the Russian soldier still standing at attention near the bow of their ship. "That poor soul," she said, keeping her voice low as they passed by. "I'm sure he's the same one who was on duty when we left for Peterhof this morning. I hope someone checks every hour or so to see if he's breathing." She lightened her tone as they approached the guard at the gangway. "I'm glad this is the last time to go through this inspection."

She handed her shore pass to the man in uniform, and there was the usual wait while he solemnly reconciled her likeness to the picture inside her passport. Then, when he couldn't appear to fault it, the passport was returned and Lynda nodded her thanks. She waited halfway up the gangway for Ross and Raoul to go through the same treatment, and when they joined her she said, "That's one formality I won't be sorry to leave. Leningrad's a great place to visit, but . . ." She paused suggestively.

Raoul frowned when Ross started to laugh. "What's so funny about that?"

"It doesn't translate," Ross replied, still chuckling. "An American proverb usually quoted by people visiting Manhattan for the first time." Then he waved in response to a hail from the deck above them. "Margareta! We were wondering if you were aboard."

"That's putting it mildly," Lynda murmured for his ears alone.

"Behave yourself," he reproved. His tone changed as he called up to the Finnish woman. "Are you coming down to join us?"

"If she does," Lynda muttered, "I'm not getting close to the rail. Ouch! What are you doing . . . ?"

Ross had put his arm around her shoulders to give her a hard squeeze that appeared affectionate only from a distance. He disregarded her protest and kept his attention riveted on the upper deck.

"I'm just going to change," Margareta called down to him. "Everybody's invited to a party in the lounge before sailing. It's in honor of the Intourist officials. Some of them are aboard already."

"What are we drinking?" Raoul asked.

"Suit yourself," Margareta said. "I saw caviar on the buffet table and champagne glasses being put out."

Ross looked at Lynda inquiringly. "I guess so," she said. "I'll have to shower and change, though. It will take a while."

"Don't let it be too long," Raoul cautioned her with a grin. "The Finns and Russians are thirsty people, especially when they don't have to pick up the check."

"You're coming?" Margareta asked, still lingering by the railing.

"We'll all be there," Raoul answered for them. "Lynda wants to change."

Margareta nodded and waved. "Then I'll see you in the lounge."

"I'll go straight on down," Raoul told Ross and Lynda, his grin broadening. "There's no point in letting free wine get warm. I'll try to save a bottle for you two if you're late. We can discuss my trip to Paris then," he added to Ross in a more serious tone.

"Fine. Just let me know what your plans are." Ross loosened his clasp on Lynda's shoulders to urge her toward the stairs amidship.

She saw Raoul disappear in the direction of the lounge before retorting mildly, "I'll have bruises in the morning after that episode."

"The way you were behaving, you deserve bruising in a different part of your anatomy. There was no point in tipping your feelings to Margareta."

"Why not? I hate being a hypocrite. It was obvious from what we overheard that there's no love lost either way." She paused as they reached the top of the stairs. "I wonder if Birger came aboard for the party."

"I have a few questions myself." Ross's tone was bland. "That's why I prefer to still be on speaking terms with Margareta when we get to the champagne. Now what's wrong?" he asked, noting her downcast expression.

"Nothing. I just wish you weren't so darned reasonable all the time." She started up the stairs to the stateroom deck. "When I looked at Margareta, all I could remember was the way she dismissed me as a 'passing affair' of yours." Lynda tried to sound nonchalant, but she waited eagerly for his denial.

Ross didn't cooperate. "You know better, so why let it rile you?" was all he said.

"Because I'm human," she snapped back.

"I thought we all came in that category." He kept his tone low as they threaded their way down the narrow corridor past the other passengers returning from a day ashore. "You're just tired. You'll feel better after a shower and some champagne."

Lynda wasn't pleased to have it confirmed that she looked as bad as she suspected. She pulled up in front of her stateroom door and found her key. "I may skip the party," she began, and found her ego somewhat restored by his sudden frown. "Actually, I don't feel much like champagne and caviar. If they were giving away chocolate milk shakes, I'd be tempted."

"If there were cheeseburgers, I'd be in line ahead of you." Ross's sympathetic grin showed that he understood.

Her anger faded, and she smiled up at him as he lingered in the corridor. "I'm being childish again. Sorry, I *must* be tired."

"But you'll come?" he urged.

"Of course she'll come." Margareta swept up beside them and gave Lynda a warm smile. "How often can you attend a farewell party in Leningrad?" Without giving her time to answer, she continued, "Birger asked me to convey a message, and I forgot to tell you when you came aboard. Ross mentioned that he'd seen us in the parking lot, didn't he?"

Lynda murmured that he said something about it.

"I thought he would. Birger was sorry he couldn't come aboard for a farewell drink, but he had a business appointment in town. Anyhow"—she rested carefully manicured fingers on Lynda's wrist—"he said to tell you that he had left the drawings and sales-promotion brochures for Arusha's new stoneware campaign at your hotel in Helsinki. He was afraid he wouldn't be back in Finland before you left for home. His ideas are something quite new, and he's convinced the Arusha people to stage a trial promotion in the States if they can find a sponsoring chain of stores. Birger says that if American consumers accept the designs, they're sure to be successful in Europe and the Commonwealth, too."

"These drawings . . ." Lynda had to swallow before she could get the word out, and she kept her glance away from Ross. "Do these drawings have to be returned?"

"I don't know." A frown played over the Finnish woman's classic features. "He didn't say. I suppose he could retrieve them when he's in New York. That won't be long—he spends most of his life on airplanes." Her expression was rueful. "That's what made so many difficulties in our personal lives. But now we have talked again"—she smiled almost shyly—"I think we will marry, after all."

There was a moment of astounded silence while Ross and Lynda just stared at her. Then Ross recovered first and leaned over to drop a quick kiss on her cheek. "That's wonderful, Margareta! Birger's a lucky man—you must tell him I said so."

"And give him my congratulations as well. You both have my very best wishes," Lynda said, even as she wondered how either of them could hope to achieve happiness if they were mixed up in the Saari affair. Margareta must have persuaded Birger to try to find a new livelihood for their future together. Perhaps the new Arusha promotion was part of it. On the other hand, his promotional drawings were too much of a coincidence to be ignored. She planned to look through every inch of them before taking the papers anywhere. Just then

Margareta's laughter made her look up in confusion.

"Anyone would think you were the prospective bride," Margareta teased. "You were miles away."

"There's nothing like the mention of a wedding to make a woman go starry-eyed," Ross agreed. "It's too bad we won't be around when the great day takes place, but perhaps you can make Birger's New York trip a honeymoon as well. I imagine you won't want to continue working with Timo Mäki after this."

Margareta's happy expression faded. "Why do you say that? Timo is a very considerate employer."

Ross refused to be riled. "I'm sure of it, but most grooms prefer to have their brides near at hand. I know I would—and that job of yours is pretty demanding."

Few women could have withstood his pleasant declaration, and Margareta was no exception. She ran a hand through her pale hair with an unconsciously preening gesture. "That is true. Perhaps you are right. I will hear what Birger has to say when the time for decisions arrives. But speaking of time . . ." She glanced at the tiny watch on her wrist and grimaced with horror. "It is so late. I must change, or the party will be over."

"Lynda was on the way to the shower, too," Ross said.

"She still is," that young woman replied, thankful for the easy exit line. "I'll see you all in the lounge a little later. Be sure and save me a glass of champagne if Raoul forgets."

Once inside her stateroom, Lynda unloaded her purchases from the Beriozhka on the dressing table. She resisted the urge to unwrap and admire them, knowing that it would take far too much time. That pleasure could be postponed until later. As she started taking off her dress, she remembered that Ross's caviar must still be with her belongings. She'd have to remember to take it with her to the party.

Once she was wrapped in her thin terry shift that doubled as a swimsuit coverup, she went in to turn on the shower. The water gushed out from the overhead fixture, and she stood out of range while she carefully adjusted the temperature. Her first hours aboard the *Borg* had shown that the hot-water supply was abundant and scalding hot. Passengers could fill hot-water bottles or even make instant coffee without ringing for the stewardess. They could also get parboiled if they weren't careful, Lynda decided when she was fiddling with the shower faucets. After a minute or two she achieved the nice warm balance she wanted and shed her wrap. She hung it on the back of the shower door and stepped halfway into the cubicle before she glanced into the soap dish on the wall and saw it was empty.

"Damn!" she murmured softly, and pushing the curtain aside, moved back into the main part of the bathroom. A survey of the washbasin showed there was no soap there either; apparently the stewardess had forgotten to bring the new supply when she brought the towels.

Drops of water from Lynda's wet body dripped onto the floor and puddled around her feet. With resignation she pulled her wrap back on and slid her feet into thongs. There was no sense leaving a trail of water all over the stateroom while she unearthed some soap from her suitcase. She reached over to turn off the shower and then decided to let it run. It would only take a minute before she'd be back.

The search took longer than she anticipated, as the plastic soap dish had hidden itself under her cosmetic bag instead of staying in its proper place. Lynda shook her head with annoyance and picked up the bar of soap. By then she was shivering in the cool air of the cabin, and it was a relief to head back toward the warmer bathroom.

As she opened the door, an onslaught of steam gushed into the stateroom. She gasped and stepped back, unable to believe that the cubicle had been transformed into an actual Turkish bath in the interval. The atmosphere started to clear as she kept the door open, but she could see new clouds of steam erupting steadily from behind the shower curtain, where the water was running. She took a deep breath and plunged into the room, planning to shut off the faucets, but when she pulled open the shower curtain, a billow of heat from the boiling water made her drop back fast.

Just then there was a commotion in the hall,

when Ross put his shoulder to her door, forcing it open with a splintering crash.

"Lynda! Are you all right?" He charged across the threshold, his hoarse cry trailing off as he saw her staring dazedly back at him from the middle of the room.

"The hot water . . . I can't turn it off," was all she could manage to say as she pulled her robe around her quaking form.

"You're not . . . ?" He had to swallow and start again. "You're not hurt?"

"No—I was hunting for something." Just then she couldn't even remember what it was. "But I can't turn the faucet off," she complained, starting back into the steam to show him.

He was beside her in an instant, to pull her back and slam the bathroom door. "The hell with that. They're working on the plumbing out in the corridor now. I was walking by when the stewardess discovered the cold-water valve had been shut off for this stateroom. Then we heard the shower running in here. God! I didn't know what we'd find." He dragged a shaking hand across his forehead. "They should have the hot water turned off any minute now."

As if in response, there was a metallic clanking out in the corridor, and abruptly the cascade of water in the shower diminished until it was a mere trickle. A moment later, even that stopped.

Ross pushed Lynda aside while he investigated the steam-filled room. Then he went back in the hall and held a low-voiced conversation with whoever was there. It wasn't long before he came back in the stateroom and shut the door firmly behind him. "I told them you were okay," he said, sounding a little more normal. He gave her a searching glance that took in her pale face and shivering frame before saying, "But I'm not sure if I am. I haven't been so damned scared in years."

Lynda couldn't remember who made the first move after that. All she knew was that his arms opened, and she flew into them, to be caught in a hard, bruising clasp against his firm body. He held her tightly until her shivering stopped. Then he raised his head and pushed her back just far enough to look down into her troubled eyes. "It wasn't an accident," he reported in a carefully level voice. "Somebody had deliberately turned off the cold water in this stateroom at the valve in the corridor."

"And if I hadn't gotten out to get the soap . . ."

The shudder that went through her body made him swear under his breath and pull her close against him again. "You're not to think of it," he ordered her fiercely. "Tomorrow we'll be back in Helsinki, and as soon after that as it can be managed, you'll be out of Finland as well."

Lynda decided that arguing was beyond her just then. Even if she had been disposed to ask if he were going with her, there was something in Ross's voice that warned her against it. He made his authority even more evident when he tilted her chin so that she had to look up at him. "You'll notice, my girl, that I'm not asking," he said. "I'm telling."

She just had time to nod slightly before his mouth came down to cover hers—as if he'd chosen to blot out all that had gone before in the best way he knew.

It was natural reaction and relief that triggered Lynda's strong response. She shuddered with sensual delight as his hands moved slowly, possessively down her back to rest on her hips. Then she was only aware of his gentle kiss that lingered and hardened, until her lips surrendered and parted under his demands.

After that, her rational thoughts ceased. It was easier that way, and there were other things for a woman to do.

Chapter Nine

All the benisons of the spring season were in evidence when the *Borg* was brought alongside her dock near Helsinki's market square the next morning. There were people everywhere enjoying the sunshine and salt breezes; office workers on their way downtown took time to admire the sleek lines of the cruise ship as they passed, porters shed their coats while they waited on the concrete loading area to transfer the passengers' luggage, and smiling immigration official joked with ship's officers as docking lines were made secure.

The nearby market square was alive with color. Flower stalls showed the bright red of geraniums mingled with purple and white petunias as gardeners inspected the best buys in bedding plants. Music blared forth from the coffee stall at the edge of the dock, where early shoppers jostled cheerfully for sweet rolls and steaming mugs of coffee.

Lynda, who was standing at the *Borg*'s rail beside Ross, was struck by the contrast with the pier in Leningrad. "It's so alive here. Bright and cheerful—noisy and relaxed. Strange that I didn't notice it before. I don't think I'll ever take such things for granted again," she added softly.

"You will. But you'll remember for a little while, and that's important." He craned his head to check the gangway. "It looks as if the luggage is going ashore now, so it shouldn't be long until they let the rest of the passengers off. Raoul wanted me to tell you that he'll see you in Copenhagen. It's going to be a close plane connection for him here."

Lynda nodded while she watched the porters trudging up and down the gangway. "He didn't think it was strange that I missed the party last night?"

"Not at all. He agreed that sightseeing could be the very devil."

"And Margareta?" Despite herself, Lynda's voice was flat. "Was she brokenhearted, too?"

Ross shook his head. "I don't know. Most of the time she was talking to some Intourist official, and after the party she disappeared. Probably ordered dinner in her stateroom, the way you did." His eyes narrowed as he watched Lynda's face. "You think she was responsible?"

Lynda maintained a carefully bland expression. "I don't know. She had the best chance to shut that water off. Plenty of time and opportunity. Of course, there were other people in the corridor . . ." She made an apologetic gesture after her voice trembled. "Sorry, those pills you gave me certainly made me sleep, but I feel as if I'll come apart at the seams if you even raise your voice."

He took her arm and turned away from the rail. "Then I'll speak softly all the way to the hotel. Once we're there, you can call Finnair and make reservations on the first flight to Copenhagen. Their ticket clerks won't do a thing to upset you." He reached out to open a door amidships. "Do you have everything from your stateroom?"

She nodded. "I'm all set to go ashore. Do we get our luggage on the pier?"

"That's right. We'll detour through immigration and customs with it, and with any luck, be on our way."

"And what about Margareta?"

"Ross's glance hardened. "I think we've been diplomatic with that young woman long enough. Certainly there's no need to hunt her up."

Lynda was relieved that the closest they came to an encounter was a brief glimpse of Margareta when they were getting into their taxi for the hotel. The Finnish woman was just then coming down the gangway, and beyond a casual glance and wave, made no attempt to communicate with them.

Ross appeared to be taking no chances when they arrived at the hotel, however. He had his bags sent to his room and escorted Lynda to hers personally along with the bellhop. Once that young man was tipped and sent on his way, Ross turned to her and said, "Okay, you make the plane reservations. I have an appointment this morning that I can't break, but after that, I'll clear the decks."

"Should I get two reservations?"

Her meek query caught him halfway to the door. He spun around with a frown. "Of course. Now, what in the merry hell do you mean by a question like that?"

His obvious annoyance was the best thing that could have happened to Lynda's spirit just then. When he had taken her in his arms the night before, he hadn't said anything about what the future might hold for the two of them.

Her distress must have communicated itself to Ross, because suddenly his frown faded, to be replaced with a whimsical expression as he reached over and pulled her close to him. "I made a vow that I wasn't going to touch you this morning," he said, giving her a gentle nip on the ear. "This isn't the place, for one thing."

"What's the other thing?"

"None of your business," he growled, fully aware of the provocation in her voice. Deliberately he put her at arm's length and shook her gently. "It's dangerous to be too close to you," he added. Then: "What's all this waffling about two tickets?" As she kept her eyes on his shirt button, he muttered awkwardly, "There isn't time to go into a hearts-and-flowers routine. You know that."

"It needn't take long." Her lashes fluttered upward. "That is, if your intentions . . ."

"My intentions are so damned honorable that I'm a nervous wreck after being around you this long." He punctuated that announcement with a quick, hard kiss. Then he dropped his arms and started for the door. "When we get to Denmark,

we'll see about making it legal. Let me know
about the reservations, and don't waste any time."
As she stood transfixed in the middle of the room
where he'd left her, he added softly, "That is . . .
if you agree. Do you, darling?"

There was a glow of happiness surrounding
Lynda like an aura, and Ross didn't really need to
hear her tremulous, "Oh, yes!" before he winked
and closed the door behind him.

Lynda stared after him with the dazed expression of a woman who has just seen the portals of
heaven open in front of her but still can't believe
the miracle. She raised her fingers to her mouth as
she finally walked over to the window to stare
down at the landscaped grounds below. Her lips
quivered under her touch, still pulsing from the
memory of Ross's possessive kiss. Then she smiled
softly, knowing that she'd better get used to such
abrupt, decisive gestures, since she planned to
spend the rest of her life with him.

A slight frown crossed her features as she
thought about his last comment, and then the
laughter lines at the corners of her lashes deepened. Of course he was serious about getting married in Denmark—and what's more, she knew him
well enough by now that he wouldn't brook any
interference on that score. Which would be the
story of their life together, she mused. Ross would
be fair enough to listen and respect her point of
view—but the final decisions would be his.

Her dreaming gaze focused suddenly on the sign
for the Finnair office just a short block away, and

she came back to reality with a vengeance. This was no day for filling mental hope chests—she had work to do.

A few minutes on the phone was long enough to have a reservations clerk tentatively promise two spaces on the Copenhagen flight in the middle of the afternoon. If she could call back shortly, she would be able to confirm it for Miss Garrett and Mr. Buchanan. Lynda thanked her and told her the number at which she could be reached. When the telephone rang a few minutes later, she thought the airline was returning the call and was surprised to hear a man's voice identifying himself as the hotel porter.

"We've been holding a small package for you, Miss Garrett," he said in passable English. "The clerk should have given it to you when you checked in this morning. May I send it up now?"

Lynda drew in her breath sharply. "Just a moment, please. What kind of a package?"

He sounded puzzled. "Some papers, I believe. A Mr. Lindh brought it by several days ago and requested that it be given to you when you returned to Helsinki. Is there anything wrong?"

Only an overactive feminine imagination, Lynda was tempted to say. Aloud she murmured, "No, of course not. If you could bring it up, I'd be very grateful."

"I shall send it with one of the boys," he replied stiffly, his tone indicating that he, personally, had better things to do.

The young man who knocked on her door a few

minutes later made up for any discourtesy, bowing gently as he handed over a thick notebook-sized package wrapped in heavy paper. Lynda smiled and tipped him, a gesture which brought forth an even deeper bow. She had to catch herself from echoing it before she closed the door. Anyone watching would have thought they were at a performance of *The Mikado,* she thought with a rueful grin.

The amusement on her face faded, however, as she surveyed the package in her hands. She carried it over to the desk against the wall and carefully removed the manila wrappings with fingers that trembled. When she uncovered an unexciting black notebook containing a thick folio of sales-presentation pieces, she uttered a soft "Damn!" of self-reproach. Birger had said he would send exactly that—so why had she thought he would enclose the mysterious drawings he and Margareta were talking about at the Beriozhka? It was no wonder that Ross was cautioning her about an overactive imagination.

Even as she was chastising herself, she was leafing through the notebook. The drawings were well-executed, but they simply showed a new design of stoneware, and even the most impartial observer would be hard put to find anything sinister in their artistic content.

Lynda had reached the final page when the telephone rang again. This time it was the clerk from Finnair to confirm the space she had requested. Lynda was just congratulating herself on how smoothly everything was going when the clerk asked for the number of Mr. Buchanan's airline ticket.

"I haven't the faintest idea," Lynda said after a moment. "Can't he give you that information when we check in for the flight?"

"I *am* sorry," the soft voice responded, "but his reservation cannot be confirmed without a ticket number, and in such a busy season . . ." Her words trailed off significantly.

"Oh, heavens, don't release the space." Lynda clutched a handful of hair as she tried to think. "Perhaps I can get in touch with him. He must be around somewhere."

The clerk sounded more cheerful. "If you could call back within fifteen minutes and ask for me, I'll hold the reservations until then."

"I'll do it. Thanks very much." Lynda hung up and then promptly dialed the hotel operator. "May I speak to Mr. Buchanan, please?"

"Mr. Buchanan? I'll ring his room." There was a prolonged ringing, then the operator's voice again. "I'm sorry . . . he doesn't answer. Is there a message?"

"Well, yes—this is Miss Garrett. I'm a friend of Mr. Buchanan's." Lynda thought that was as good a way to put it as any. "It's terribly important that I get in touch with him."

"Miss Garrett?" The operator's voice warmed perceptibly. "Mr. Buchanan left special instructions if you called. He can be reached up at the roof sauna—I'll put you through."

The phone buzzed again while Lynda was still repeating "roof sauna" in a perplexed tone. The voice that answered the summons this time said something in Finnish and then switched to heavily accented English as Lynda asked for Mr. Buchanan.

"He's here . . . but it is not possible for me to get him at this moment. You understand?"

"I think so. . . ." Lynda made a quick decision. "Look, I'll come up. It's necessary that I see him for a few minutes."

"Your name, please?"

"Lynda Garrett. Tell him not to go away." She hung up without waiting for an answer to that, and pausing only to clutch her purse and room key, headed for the elevator. When it arrived, she checked the control buttons and then pressed the one marked "roof sauna–swimming pool."

As the doors parted a minute later on the top floor, a strong smell of chlorine greeted her. She walked down a corridor to an empty receptionist's desk with a beige telephone and appointment pad atop it. Lynda hovered for a moment or two and then moved slowly down an even narrower corridor with numbered doors on one side of it. She debated knocking on one which was slightly ajar, and finally decided against it. Just then a glass door at the end of the corridor opened, and Lynda saw Ross's familiar form. He said something over his shoulder before he turned and recognized her.

The sudden warmth that came into his expression would have convinced her of his love even if she'd had any reason to doubt it, and it was difficult to subdue an impulse to throw herself into his arms.

Ross came up with an acceptable compromise; he reached out to put a possessive arm around her shoulders and dropped a quick kiss on her nose. "I heard you were looking for me. What's happening, my love?"

She swallowed and smiled back at him, wondering if she'd ever get used to the delicious feeling that stole over her every time he came within reach.

Her feelings must have been evident in her glance, because he brushed another quick kiss—this time over her cheekbone—and said roughly, "You'll have to stop looking at me like that, or we'll be thrown out of here."

She wrinkled her nose. "What do you mean?"

"The Finns are particular about behavior in their saunas." He waved a hand at the closed doors. "It's all very proper and aboveboard in there."

"Good heavens, is that what those doors lead to?" She was horrified. "I almost peeked in one when I couldn't find anybody around."

He started to laugh. "It's a good thing you didn't."

"But what are you doing here?"

"Believe it or not, I had an appointment with a hotelman up here a little while ago."

"In a sauna?" She was incredulous.

"Actually, I met him for coffee by the swimming pool, but the Finns think nothing of holding meetings at the sauna. Politicians have even scheduled cabinet meetings in them. They claim that antagonism melts in the heat, and any protocol disappears when people shed their clothes. It's hard to be dignified when you're clutching a bath towel." He looked more closely at her. "But you didn't come along to learn about saunas. Have you had some bad news?"

"Not really." Suddenly she remembered why she was there. "The airline wants your ticket number for the Copenhagen flight this afternoon. They need it before they can confirm the space."

"I'll phone in right away. Anything else happen?"

"Just that the package from Birger arrived. The one Margareta mentioned on the ship."

"And?"

Her hands went out in a scrubbing gesture. "Nothing that I can see—a simple sales presentation for Arusha. The porter said that it arrived a couple days ago."

"So it all fits." He explained as she glanced questioningly at him, "When I met the fellow for coffee a little while ago, he brought up Birger's name during our conversation. He thought Birger might be good at handling convention-arrangement details for me in Scandinavia if Raoul needs assistance. The word's out that Birger quit his designing post at Arusha this past week, and he's looking for a job."

There was a worried frown on Lynda's face as

she considered the news. "That fits in with what
we overheard in Leningrad. Maybe Margareta's
convinced him to get away from Helsinki so that
their marriage has a chance. I wish I knew what it
was all about."

"So do I." His concerned glance lingered on
her. Then he said impulsively, "What do you have
scheduled for the next hour or so?"

"Nothing special. Why? Is there something you
want me to do?"

"Uh-huh." He started leading her back to the
reception desk. "You might as well take a health
cure. You'll be finished with a sauna and the
washerwoman by the time I make some phone calls.
Then we can have a late lunch and head for the
airport. How does that sound?"

"As if you're going too fast," she protested, pulling up before they reached a blond woman now
seated at the receptionist's desk. "I didn't even
bring a swimsuit with me."

"You don't need one." When she looked doubt-
ful, he grinned reassuringly. "Leave it all to me.
You can't leave Finland without indulging in their
national pastime."

Lynda didn't argue any longer. After all that
had happened, most anything would be an improvement. Besides, she was curious. "All right,
I'm game," she said. "What's this about a washerwoman?"

"I'll explain after I've arranged it all. Don't go
away."

She shook her head and then pretended to examine the paintings on the walls of the corridor while Ross arranged the appointment. From the blond's expression it was evident that she wasn't immune to his persuasion. She ran a finger up and down the appointment sheet and nodded before reaching for the phone at her elbow.

"You're all set with the second shift," Ross said, coming back to Lynda. "The receptionist will call me when you're finished, and I'll pick you up."

Lynda caught his arm when he started to push open one of the dressing-room doors for her. "What's this about a second shift?"

His grin was teasing. In the old times, men took the first shift, women the second, and the elves were allotted the third. There's even a Finnish spell attributed to the sauna elf's bridal charm."

Lynda's eyebrows went up. "I'd like to hear more about that."

"Another time," he said hastily. "Of course, in those days, brides were given saunas before they went to the church ceremony, and later on in their marriage they used the sauna to cure meat and dry the family's flax or hemp. All you have to do to-day, though, is relax and enjoy the treatment."

"What does the washerwoman have to do with it?"

"Don't look so suspicious. It's perfectly above-board. She's a dignified middle-aged lady who comes in and sloshes warm water over you before scrubbing every inch of your skin with a loofah sponge. She's seen so many naked people in her work that there's nothing to be embarrassed about." He gave her a gentle push through the door. "Now, get going. You'll feel great afterward, and you can thank me later. Someplace where there aren't so many chaperons."

Chapter Ten

At it happened, there was scarcely time to discuss anything before they were bused out to the Helsinki airport later in the day. Even the lunch Ross mentioned had been open-faced sandwiches eaten hastily in the downtown air terminal.

Ross had their luggage checked in before joining Lynda at the stand-up sandwich bar on the balcony. "Sorry about this rush, but it couldn't be helped," he said.

"It doesn't matter a bit." She offered him the open-faced cheese sandwich she'd selected for him while he was busy at the ticket counter. "I hope that's okay. There wasn't much choice; it was either cheese or sardines."

"Cheese is fine." He took a bite and reached for his coffee to wash it down. "I don't know why people on this side of the Atlantic make nasty remarks about American hamburgers. In Britain, they eat cheese-and-tomato sandwiches all day; in Paris, it's cheese and French bread. The Germans give you cheese and a hard roll, and in Scandinavia they put the same cheese on one slice of bread . . ."

"And charge you twice as much for it." She smiled sympathetically. "You sound as if you've had a bad morning."

"Just a busy one. I didn't mean to grouse." He let his masculine gaze run over her in a way that made her color rise. "That sauna therapy worked," he said. "You look wonderful."

"A visit to the hairdresser helped," she confessed. "My hairdo took the count under all that heat and water."

"Well, I like the end result. Did I ever mention that you're an extremely tasty dish?"

"I think you have me confused with the cheese sandwich," she replied solemnly.

"I may have, at that." He glanced at his watch. "Let's sort it out on the flight. That's our bus they're calling now."

Lynda took a last sip of coffee and picked up her coat and leather tote bag. "Do you want me to carry anything?" She was watching him tuck two attaché cases and a newspaper under his arm. "I could help with that carry-on stuff."

"No, thanks. I can manage." He led the way to the outer door of the air terminal and held it open for her. An airport bus was waiting at the curb with its motor running. The driver smiled and nodded as they came aboard, waited for them to get seated halfway back, and then was waved on by the dispatcher.

Ross put his attaché cases on an empty seat across the aisle and deposited Lynda's belongings next to them as the bus went out to the Manner-

heimintie and turned left on the busy thoroughfare. "We were lucky to escape overweight charges
with all that stuff," Ross said, sitting back down
again. "I hope we're as lucky when we fly home—
especially after shopping in Denmark."

She glanced across at his belongings to ask, "Are
you important enough to rate two briefcases all the
time?"

"Hardly. Blame the extra one on Raoul. Also an
extra suitcase. He didn't want to carry them to
Paris and back again to Denmark tomorrow, so I
took pity on him. If we can't find a porter at the
Copenhagen airport, I may live to regret it." Ross's
voice showed that it didn't really bother him. His
glance was trained just then on the imposing
Olympic stadium they were passing, and the well-
kept grounds around it. "Sorry to be leaving Helsinki?"

"In a way." Her voice took on a shy note, and
she avoided his eyes. "But I'm looking forward to
Denmark tremendously."

"In more ways than one." His hand covered hers
in a possessive clasp. "From now on, all the memo-
ries will be good ones. First thing you'll have to do
in Copenhagen is phone your boss and tell him
you're taking time off for a honeymoon." He
grinned down at her. "We can argue about
whether you go back to work later. You'll notice
that I'm being diplomatic and not issuing any ulti-
matums."

"You should. At this moment, I don't care if I
ever see another set of stoneware in my life. Once I

turn in Birger's package"—she nodded toward her tote bag—"I think I'll find another line of work. Do you need a new secretary?"

Ross's features softened, and the way he looked at her made Lynda catch her breath. He pulled her hand onto his thigh and held it there as he said, "I'd prefer a wife."

"I hoped you might," she managed finally, wondering if she could be heard over the thunder of her heartbeat.

"Good, that's settled." Then, as she started to laugh softly, he said, "Now what's struck your fancy?"

"Imagine being proposed to on an airport bus," she told him. "What will our grandchildren think?"

"They should be so lucky. Just for that, I'll do it again in Tivoli Gardens. That should satisfy all the romantic conventions. In the meantime, you can read the Copenhagen guidebook during our flight and decide what you want to see on our honeymoon."

"What are you going to be doing while I'm reading the guidebook?"

He yawned and stretched. "Taking a nap. I'll need all my strength to find out how quickly two Americans can get married in Copenhagen, once we arrive."

Lynda was a little surprised after takeoff to find that Ross meant to do exactly that. He extracted a pillow from the stewardess, pushed back his aisle seat so that he could get comfortable, told Lynda to "get cracking" with her reading, and closed his eyes. He slept so soundly that she had to waken him an hour and a half later when the seatbelt sign came on for their descent at Copenhagen.

"How do you do it?" Lynda asked him admiringly as he stretched and pushed a button on his armrest to bring his seat upright again. "I'm so busy helping the pilot that I can never close an eye on an airplane."

"There's no need for everybody to watch the wings and make sure they don't fall off," he reported with a lazy grin.

"I don't know about that. It's hard work to watch the wings and make sure there aren't any flames shooting out of the engines at the same time. I was hardly able to get my reading done," she reported, leaning over to tuck the guidebook into her bag by her feet.

Ross peered over her shoulder to check the weather as the plane banked on its final approach. "At least you didn't have to worry about the pilot colliding with a mountain around here. Did you ever see anything so flat as this countryside?"

"And sunshine, too." Lynda gave a small sigh of content. "Something tells me I'm going to like Denmark."

When they deplaned a little later, her hopes were confirmed. The airport personnel greeted them with smiles, passenger-arrival areas were clearly marked, and English signs were posted everywhere. There was even a waiting taxi after they had cleared with the genial Danish immigration and customs men. The latter had taken a cursory

look at their passports and waved them through
the barrier after the briefest of inspections.

"A little different from Leningrad," Lynda said
as they followed their porter to the cabstand.

"In more ways than one," Ross concurred. "Just
wait and see."

On the twenty-minute ride into the heart of the
city, he went over Lynda's list of places that she
especially wanted to see. "I'll have to check in at
the embassy first thing," he told her. "There's a
pal of mine who might be able to cut some red
tape for us. I'm not sure whether Americans have
to observe the same waiting period for marriage
ceremonies as the Danes."

"Should I go with you . . . to the embassy, I
mean?"

"I don't think it's necessary on the first visit."
He rubbed his chin thoughtfully. "Why don't you
find something interesting to do for an hour or so.
Something that does *not* involve asking any more
street directions from strange men," he added
sternly.

"All right, if you insist." She kept her tone as
solemn as his. "But I had awfully good luck the
first time."

He shot a quick glance at the driver before ad-
ministering a chastising pinch on the closest part
of her anatomy. Her surprised protest was ignored,
but her unrepentant chuckle of laughter which followed wasn't. "I'll extract a proper punishment later," he threatened. Then he took the guidebook
from her unresisting fingers and leafed through it.

"After we check in at the hotel, why don't you take a canal cruise? It's a good way to get your bearings in the city. When I get back from the embassy, we can visit the Little Mermaid statue together. Afterward we'll call on the rector at the English church in the same part of town. How does that sound?"

"Heavenly," she breathed, wondering how Ross had escaped seeing the rector of a church before this, and giving silent thanks that it hadn't happened until she came along.

Ross gave her a whimsical, considering look and relaxed on the seat beside her, as if he, too, was more than content with his lot.

Their hotel was a modern skyscraper which overlooked Tivoli and was close to the Market Square. The reservation clerk welcomed them politely, assigned them rooms on the same floor, and then came back empty-handed after searching for keys. "I'm so sorry," he told them. "The rooms aren't ready yet. We've been solidly booked for the past week with an international convention, and some of the guests were late in checking out. The maids should have your rooms ready in another hour at the most. If you care to wait in the lobby, or perhaps the coffee shop . . ." He gestured toward an alcove beyond the elevators.

"We'll manage, thanks," Ross told him. He took Lynda by the elbow and steered her over to the porter's desk to check on the luggage. The man in charge assured him that their baggage could be left piled against a nearby pillar.

"As soon as your rooms are ready, I'll have it taken up," he promised.

Ross didn't look happy, but there didn't appear to be any other choice. He gave the luggage a second look over his shoulder as he and Lynda moved to the center of the luxurious lobby.

Her glance was already roaming the shop windows around them. "What gorgeous displays! Are those mink coats over there?"

Ross rolled his eyes heavenward. "Lord, what am I getting into? We should never have left Helsinki!"

"I don't know why not," she told him demurely. "I tried a sauna—now I'm ready for something else. Besides, there's still time for you to change your mind."

"Not on your life." He sounded gratifyingly emphatic. "We'll window-shop for your wedding present later." He bent to give her a quick kiss. "I'll phone your room when I return from the embassy. Don't get lost on your canal cruise in the meantime. Okay?"

She nodded. "I'll be careful. Hurry back."

His tall figure disappeared through the broad lobby door. Lynda stifled a sigh, telling herself that it was foolish to feel suddenly bereft because Ross wasn't within sight. She wasn't altogether successful in assuming an air of determined cheerfulness as she went back to the porter's desk. "Could you tell me where I take the boat for the canal cruise?"

"Of course, miss. The easiest way is to get a cab

from here. Just give the doorman this address." He was scribbling on a card. "The boats leave each half-hour, so you shouldn't have to wait long."

"Thank you." She took the card he handed her. "And you will keep an eye on the luggage while I'm gone."

"Certainly, miss. No need to worry."

"I suppose not, but . . . " She frowned and then said impulsively, "I'd better take the smaller pieces with me—those two attaché cases can be stuffed in the side of my tote bag." She gestured toward the luggage as she spoke. "It's hard to keep track of smaller things, and they keep sliding off the pile." She didn't mention that she'd already seen one of Ross's attaché cases carelessly pushed over by a hurrying passerby.

"Whatever you say, miss." It was clear the porter thought she was being difficult, but hotel training kept his feelings well-cloaked. "The suitcases are sure to be in your rooms by the time you come back from the canal trip."

"Fine, thanks." Lynda went over to collect the two attaché cases and stuff them in the side of her soft tote bag. When she was finished, the result was bulky but still manageable by slinging the long leather straps of the travel bag over her shoulder. She made sure that the Copenhagen guidebook was easily available in a side pocket before heading for the door.

The card that the porter had given her acted like a charm; the doorman smiled and nodded before signaling to a waiting cab. He opened the door for Lynda and gave some directions in Danish to the driver. A minute later she was on her way. Traffic was heavy in the downtown area, but the city thoroughfares were wide, and cars moved swiftly. Lynda attempted to identify some of the passing buildings from the pictures in the guidebook but soon gave up and simply settled back to enjoy the excitement.

A little later, the driver turned left onto a street which hugged the banks of a good-sized canal. Narrow two-story shop buildings with stone fronts marched solidly on the far side, and up on the right Lynda could see the rococo tower of the Stock Exchange, one of the famous landmarks of the city. The entwined tails of four dragons on the steeple made the world's first securities market easy to identify. All around it the green oxidized-copper roofs that were Copenhagen's trademark added a colorful touch to the legendary buildings.

Lynda was so engrossed in the panorama that she scarcely realized when the driver pulled to the curb. He turned in his seat to get her attention and pointed to the canal below. An open sightseeing craft which had been drawn up to a stone landing at the bottom of some steep steps was filling steadily with toursits.

"Thanks, I understand." Lynda glanced at the meter and rummaged for her change purse to find some Danish kroner, thankful that she'd changed money at the airport when they arrived. The amount she handed over must have been satisfactory, because the driver opened her door smartly and pulled at the brim of his cap as she got out. Then, so there could be no possible misunderstanding, he even pointed elaborately toward the canal-cruise ticket booth at the top of the steps.

Lynda nodded and started for a stone bridge crossing the canal some twenty feet away, thinking as she walked that she'd better check her currency-conversion table again. Cabdrivers, no matter what country, were only that obliging when they were magnificently overpaid.

Fortunately, the admission price for the canal boat cruise was prominently posted, and the woman selling tickets in the booth spoke excellent English. She confirmed that the trip lasted approximately an hour, and taxis would be available on their return. She also suggested that Lynda get aboard promptly, because the deckhand was even then waiting to cast off.

Lynda caught up her ticket and hurried down the stone steps. After she had settled at the end of a crowded bench on the boat, she realized that she needn't have hurried quite so much, because another group of tourists was still loading at the stern. At that moment, the attractive blond tour guide took up her microphone and started to bid them welcome in French, German, and English. Lynda wondered fleetingly which translation the Japanese man beside her was listening to, and then she settled back on the wooden seat as the boat moved out into mid-canal.

Before many minutes had passed, she realized that Ross had been inspired when he suggested the cruise as an introduction to Copenhagen's history and physical layout. The canal guide was well-versed in pleasing customers, and imparted information in a friendly manner, unlike some other foreign guides Lynda had endured, who spoke English in hoarse, undecipherable accents, snarled statistics, and obviously wished foreigners would stay home. Halfway through those tours, naturally, all foreigners were wishing exactly the same thing.

The attractive Danish guide gently explained that it was the water crossroads location which gave the capital city its name eight hundred years before—Köbenhavn, or "Merchants' Harbor." The center subsequently grew to the current metropolis, with twenty-five miles of quays, where three hundred fifty ships could be berthed simultaneously.

The cruise boat plowed steadily through the smooth water, nudging past the blocks full of warehouses where goods in transit were stored, and even ducking under the bow of a sleek passenger ship anchored at a modern pier. To the delight of everyone, the canal boat made a special slow cruise past the Little Mermaid—Copenhagen's most charming waterside statue. The bronze heroine of Hans Christian Andersen's fairy tale was the object of every camera enthusiast within sight, both aboard the boat and on the Langelinie promenade. Lynda knew that she'd returning later with Ross for a more leisurely view, so she left her camera in her tote bag and obediently moved out of the way so others could get their quota of pictures.

After the Little Mermaid, the canal boat picked up speed somewhat, and Lynda saw that the tour was almost at a close. The guide confirmed it a minute later, saying that for a final treat they would cruise the Nyhavn Canal with its picturesque eighteenth-century buildings and coffee houses that sailors still frequented when they were in port. She broke off her explanation to point out a newly designed hydrofoil carrying commuters to Malmö in Sweden.

The contrast between the old and new was emphasized even more after they left the Nyhavn Canal and the guide pointed out the ancient district of Christianshavn, where the famous steeple of Our Savior's Church was still visible over the rooftops. "And now, we'll pull up at this pier by the stone bridge," she continued, smiling. "One of our staff will come aboard to take Polaroid pictures so that you will have a memento of our cruise. There are also cold drinks and ice-cream bars to refresh you." She ignored the surprised murmur from her passengers at the unexpected delay. There were no audible comments; they were a captive audience, and they knew it. Besides, the thought of food was always appealing. "The rest stop will only be five minutes," the guide continued. "You may either stay aboard or on the dock."

Lynda looked over the fare and decided that it wasn't worth going ashore for such a short time, especially since they weren't selling any of the bright-red hot dogs that she'd seen on roadside stands earlier. While most of the other passengers clambered onto the dock, her gaze wandered lazily over the freight barge going past, and then up to the pedestrians crossing the old stone bridge spanning the canal just ahead of them.

It was the abrupt movement of a fair-haired man at the bridge railing which caught her eye first. As she recognized Birger Lindh's suddenly retreating figure, she gasped and got to her feet in alarm. By then, Birger's tall figure had moved out of her sight, and the pedestrians and cars on the bridge kept her from seeing whether he was making his way to a small stairway leading to the canal ahead of them. If he were, it would be a simple matter for him to reach the boat before the guide got the tour under way again.

Instinct made Lynda push past her Japanese neighbor with an apologetic murmur and accept a crewman's helping hand onto the stone wharf. From then on she kept her head down as she walked rapidly to another stone stairway leading to street level. Halfway up, she thought there was a shout of protest when the Danish guide discovered one of her flock escaping, but Lynda didn't look back.

She pulled up when she reached the sidewalk, wondering why there was never a cruising cab when it was really needed. Another fleeting glimpse over her shoulder revealed a tall, fair-haired man, and she hurried on across the bridge. If Birger had made his way to Copenhagen and was tracking her down on a tourist cruise, she'd make sure that he didn't catch up with her until Ross was by her side.

As Lynda made her way down the busy sidewalk, trying to keep in the middle of the clumps of pedestrians, she could easily understand how Birger might have located their trail.

Apparently Ross had often stayed at their Copenhagen hotel, and once Birger got that far, it wouldn't have taken any persuasion for the man at the porter's desk to tell him where she'd gone. Since the canal boats followed a regular tour route, all he had to do was linger calmly on the bridge to intercept her.

Lynda waited impatiently on the curb for a traffic light to change—there were small cars thronging the street, but the only taxis had passengers in them, and the drivers paid not the slightest attention to her upraised arm.

She turned to a buxom woman with a shopping bag who walked up beside her. "Excuse me . . . could you tell me where I could find a cabstand?" As the woman frowned, Lynda went on desperately, "A taxi . . . telephone . . ." The woman's frown changed to an apologetic expression, and she shook her head. When the light changed, she gave Lynda a final pitying glance before going on her way.

Lynda stood there, biting her lip in frustration, until she suddenly realized there were some Danish phrases in her guidebook. She started to rummage for it in her tote bag and then decided to keep walking as she looked.

The tolling of a nearby church bell brought her head up when she reached the far curb and she saw the tower of Our Savior's Church, which the guide had earlier pointed out as a tourist landmark. Lynda stared at it, deciding it resembled a miniature Tower of Pisa with its outside winding stair, only this structure was surmounted by a huge gilt ball. A figure of Christ holding a banner stood atop the ball, giving it a distinctive and almost bizarre appearance.

Lynda's face brightened, and she hurried along the sidewalk. The church was just the type of place where groups of tourists would congregate. And wherever there were tourists, there would be someone who spoke English or could use a telephone for her. If nothing else, she could stay in the middle of a tour group and request a ride back to town from their guide.

That thought buoyed her so much that she was almost smiling when she turned in the brick courtyard surrounding the old church. She made her way up the path to the big arched door and tugged at the wrought-iron ring in the middle of it. The heavy door didn't budge. Lynda banged her knuckles as she tried again. The church had to be open in the afternoon, she thought frantically, it just had to be. She risked another furtive look over her shoulder. Birger Lindh was standing on the far curb of the busy street which fronted the church grounds and staring directly at her. Even as she watched, there was a break in the traffic and he started across.

Lynda didn't wait any longer. She raced around the corner of the building on a path almost hidden by unpruned shrubbery. A minute later, she saw a sign with an arrow which pointed to a much smaller door—but one which stood hospitably open.

She was breathing hard as she rushed up a short flight of sagging stone steps and stepped across worn lintel. The entranceway was so dark that she had to stop and blink, trying to accustom herself to the sudden gloom.

A small desk stood at one side of the high-ceilinged room. Its top was covered with pamphlets explaining the history of the church in various languages. Next to it was a locked wooden cash box with a slit in the top and the word "Tower" written in four languages on its side. A wooden chair behind the table had a man's navy-blue suit coat folded neatly over it.

Lynda looked around desperately, trying to will the coat's owner into instant appearance. Then her glance focused on a pair of swinging doors at the end of the room, near the unswept wooden stairway which obviously led to the church tower.

She darted over to the doors and pushed one cautiously open; the dignified gloom of the church interior appeared before her in deserted and somewhat faded grandeur.

Imposing tin pipes loomed above a gigantic pipe-organ console on one wall. With its Saxon woodcarving and fan-shaped stucco decor, only the Hunchback of Notra-Dame was needed at the keyboard to terrify Lynda still more.

The marble altar which swam into her gaze next wasn't any help either. The stucco angel at its base seemed aloof, and the small angels playing on canvas above looked down on her with blank and unconcerned expressions. Stern rows of empty wooden pews blurred slightly as Lynda's eyes filled with sudden tears.

She turned and hurried out of that cold room, determined to find sanctuary elsewhere. Perhaps the guard would have reappeared by now. He wouldn't go off for long and leave a cash box unattended.

But she had only to push through the swinging doors into the vestibule to see that the verger apparently wasn't worried about the honesty of church visitors. He was still among the missing.

Lynda made some sort of exclamation and rubbed her hand over her perspiring cheeks. By then, the leather straps of her tote bag felt as if they were chain mail cutting into her shoulder, and her legs ached with hurrying. She cast a last frenzied glance around the empty anteroom and decided to take her chances out-of-doors.

It was the sudden shout of masculine voices outside which stopped her. Birger's was one . . . she was sure of it. She was also sure that the other wasn't an elderly quavering voice belonging to the owner of the navy-blue coat.

With that escape route blocked, there was only one way left. Lynda moaned like a cornered animal and slipped up the wooden stairway leading to the tower, trying to keep her leather soles from grinding on the sandy dust which layered the old stairs.

For the first few flights, the stair was wide and well-lighted by small, irregularly placed windows in the thick brick exterior. In addition, there was a wooden railing to guide her, well-polished by generations of tower visitors.

Then abruptly the windows stopped, and the only light came from bulbs which dangled at the landings. There was just enough illumination to show that the brick wall beside her was supported by hand-hewn members, which in turn, were reinforced by hand-wrought iron fastenings.

Lynda gave them a cursory glance as she paused at a dusty landing to get her breath and tried to hear if anyone was following her. Her heart was pounding so hard that it was difficult to listen properly, but when she leaned over the stair railing trying to see down, she suddenly heard the sound of firm footsteps advancing steadily from below.

That confirmation of her fears made her sway weakly, and it was instinct rather than inclination that pushed her feet on up the next flight of steps. By then she was clinging to the banister for support as the steps narrowed into a tight spiral, and the light became even feebler.

Even as Lynda struggled upward, she was wondering where it all would end. Perhaps it would be better to go back down and meet Birger on a well-lighted landing. It was absurd to imagine that anything dangerous was going to happen merely because she caught a glimpse of the man. There could be dozens of logical reasons for his presence in Copenhagen.

But if that were true, why had he followed her from the canal? And why was he shadowing her footsteps up an old church tower that had little to recommend it—unless you liked climbing wooden staircases or inspecting old clockworks. She gave the latter a brief glance as she doggedly kept moving. Then suddenly she came upon another wooden landing—this time the platform for the tower bells and the maze of wires which operated them. There was more light, too, and Lynda dazedly looked around to identify the source. It didn't take long to find it—a wooden door ajar just beyond the bell platform.

She almost cried when she saw the continuation of the inside stairway next to it—little more than a spiral ladder that looked like scaffolding in the center of the narrowing church tower.

Lynda gave a groan of despair. She'd have to see what was past the open door. Possibly there was some kind of exterior stairway leading to the ground.

She moved quickly over to the doorway and peered through, but her initial glance was enough to smash that brief moment of hope. There was an outside stair, but it only led upward from a narrow wooden widow's-walk affair which extended on either side of her. Lynda clung to its frail railing with a desperation that turned her knuckles white as she looked down on the slate rooftops of Christianshavn.

At any other time, she would have paused to admire the panorama spread out before her—the steep-pitched architecture from another era, the miniature figures of crewmen aboard the canal barges headed toward the sea and beyond, a covey of oil-storage tanks arranged like stepping-stones leading to the breakwater. The cloudless sky was a pale-blue canopy over it all with color tones as soft as an artist's wash drawing. Even the jumbo jet approaching over the sea added to the composition, illustrating the contrast between the old world and the new.

And in the midst of all those riches, Lynda could only think of one thing. There was no escape for her—no easy way out.

She turned back into the church tower and stood quietly waiting on the bell platform for the man coming up the final stairs. Now that the moment had arrived, there was even a sense of relief in the confrontation.

Raoul Bonet's abrupt appearance on the top step instead of Birger Lindh's made her collapse against the stair railing. "Oh . . . my Lord!" She was barely able to whisper the words. "Raoul! You scared me to death. I didn't dream it was you."

"Just who did you think it was, *chérie?*" He seemed amused as he moved onto the platform. "Was there a reason for bringing me to the top of this accursed place?"

"I thought it was . . ." She started to frame Birger's name, and then changed her mind as she saw his intent expression. "I thought it was some strange man behind me," she substituted quickly. "I could hear your footsteps, and . . . this place isn't exactly Times Square or Piccadilly. Not for a woman alone." Her gesture encompassed the dismal platform.

A brilliant smile creased his face. "You're quite right. Well, now you can relax and enjoy the panorama as you were meant to. I'll just pick up my property and leave you in peace."

"Your property?" She stared up at him, puzzled.

"My attaché case. I presume you have it stored in your shoulder bag." His tone taunted her. "You American women are all the same with your sensible shoes and shoulder bags large enough to carry a month's rations."

She smiled and slipped the purse strap from her shoulder as she eased the tote bag onto the dusty floor. "That's why we're all lopsided when we get back home. You'll have to tell me which attaché case is yours." Then her head came up suddenly. "How on earth did you know I had it?"

There was an instant's pause before he uttered a short laugh. "How do you suppose? I asked Ross, of course. At the hotel a little while ago."

"And he told you that I'd be here?" She frowned as she thought about it. "He knew I was taking the canal boat . . ."

"Exactly." Raoul brushed some imaginary dust from the sleeve of his sport coat. "I hate to rush you, Lynda, but I am in a bit of a hurry."

She wasn't influenced by his show of impatience. It was evident in her next remark. "But Ross didn't know I was going to come here. I didn't know it myself. The only way you could have found out was to have followed me. And I thought it was Birger . . ."

"Birger Lindh?" Raoul's attitude of forbearance disappeared like chalk under an eraser, and his new hostility made Lynda take an instinctive step backward.

"You saw Lindh?" he pressed insistently. "He was here?"

"Not here exactly. I thought I saw him at the canal landing."

"It is no matter." Swiftly Raoul bent down and rummaged through her bag. It took only seconds before he extracted a black attaché case and gave a murmur of satisfaction.

Lynda put a restraining hand on his arm when he turned to go. "Just a minute! You can't walk away with that."

"My dear girl—don't be absurd. It belongs to me. Don't interfere in things that don't concern you, Lynda. You'll find it's much safer." His glance flickered idly around the platform. "Besides, this is scarcely a place for you to make threatening gestures. As you said before, it isn't Times Square or Piccadilly. If there were to be an accident up here . . ." His uncaring shrug finished the sentence.

"Like all the other accidents?" Lynda's accusation burst out recklessly. Quite suddenly she saw that every suspicious thought she'd had regarding Birger or Margareta could have applied equally well to Raoul. And if he was so anxious to escape with the attaché case, it must be important. Too important for him to bring through Danish customs, she realized at that moment. That was why he'd begged Ross to carry it with his things. Probably the Frenchman hadn't gone to Paris at all.

Raoul's intent gaze didn't leave her face while she was doing the reasoning. The mirthless smile that finally twisted his lips showed that he'd reached his own conclusions. He came a step closer to her and said softly, "Accidents? What are you talking about, *chérie?*"

"Don't call me that!" She retreated until the plank railing which protected the bells bruised her back. "You know very well what I mean." Suddenly it seemed important for her to keep talking. She was aware that Birger had followed her to the church grounds, so he must be somewhere near. And if Raoul was wary of his presence, the Finnish designer might be there to help her. Even as she assured herself of that fact, she knew there was a hole in her logic. Birger might want the information in that attaché case for his own ends. Her mind mentally threw in the towel at that reasoning, and she shuddered noticeably.

"You don't look at all well. Perhaps if you went out where there was some air . . ." Raoul gestured toward the door leading to the widow's walk.

"No, thank you. I'd rather stay inside."

He raised his eyebrows. "I won't insist—just now." The last two words were mocking. "But I'm beginning to think that's the only answer. If you should have an accident up here, there would be no suspicion."

"Even after I've had so many near-misses in the last few days?" It was an effort to keep her voice level, but she managed. "Were you involved with that man Saari?"

"Only indirectly." The candor in his tone showed that he had no intention of letting her voice her suspicions to anyone else, and they both knew it. "It was unfortunate that you saw me in the park with Timo Mäki that morning in Helsinki," Raoul went on. "I was watching you carefully at the banquet later that night to see if you were going to give me away."

"You needn't have worried," Lynda protested truthfully. "I thought you looked vaguely familiar, but that was all."

"But you didn't waste any time getting on the ship to Leningrad with us."

"That was because of Margareta. Ross said . . ."

"I can imagine what he said." Raoul's eyebrows went up knowingly. "He wouldn't have been so amused by her pursuit if he'd realized that she was simply doing her job. Margareta has been very effective for us in the past, until that fool Birger came along to distract her. We have ways of dealing with that."

"The same technique you tried on me?" Lynda's voice wobbled a little, despite her efforts. "You were the one who came up behind me at the Hermitage, weren't you? And put me in that closet afterward."

"It was amazing how you were always underfoot," he complained. "And with all of the city of

Leningrad, you still managed to observe that fool Mäki in the one place he shouldn't have been seen. Fortunately, you weren't discreet in announcing Lindh's presence, as well."

"I'm glad to have helped," she said, trying to match his sarcasm.

"The only way you could help was to be out of commission just then. That's why you were . . . detained at the museum."

"And aboard the ship?"

His gaze was dispassionate. "By then, I had more specific orders. It was fortunate that Ross announced you were leaving Helsinki the next day. We weren't sorry to see you go."

"And now?"

Raoul's dark eyes were completely devoid of emotion as he flexed his fingers and moved slightly closer. "Now, my dear Lynda, I am sorry, but your amazing luck has run out. Your accusations would be an embarrassment to us—don't bother denying it." The last was added in a measured analytical tone as she started to protest.

A sharp peal from the bell platform behind them made both of them give a start of surprise and turn to see what was happening. The wires attached to all of the smaller bells began to move, even as they watched, and the building volume of the concert made Lynda wince and put her hands to her ears. She started for the stairs, even forgetting the man beside her in her flight from that strident discord. Raoul's arm shot out as she came abreast of him. He spun her around and thrust her cruelly ahead of him toward the narrow outside catwalk.

"This way . . . I haven't changed my plans," he shouted at her over the tumult reverberating around them. "Get up, you fool!" he added angrily as Lynda's knees gave way and she crumpled at his feet. The combination of bedlam and fear left Lynda barely aware of what she was doing, but instinct made her clutch at a rough wooden support as she went down.

Raoul tried to jerk her away with his free hand. When she tightened her grip, he swore violently and dropped the attaché case so that he could use his full strength in lifting her.

There was such a violent look of hate on his face that Lynda squeezed her eyes shut and clung like a limpet to the rough wood pillar. She braced herself for another onslaught, and when it didn't come, her eyelids opened to a frightened slit.

Raoul was being hustled roughly off the platform and down the stairs by Birger and a thickset man in uniform. At the same time, the echo of the Frenchman's curses rattling off the tower walls showed that the clamor of the bells had abruptly stopped in mid-concert.

A movement on the other side of the platform made Lynda draw in her breath sharply before she identified the man bending down to carefully retrieve Raoul's attaché case from the floor. She watched him prop it against the edge of the stairway, and then, still breathing hard from his charge up the steps, he came over to sit beside her on the dusty floor.

It took a minute before he could speak. Then Ross said, "I think we've earned a small rest before we go down."

Lynda could only stare at him. "And I think," she managed to say eventually, "that's the understatement of the year."

Chapter Eleven

"How on earth did you manage to find me?" Lynda finally asked a few minutes later.

She was almost back to normal after a brief interlude that involved resting her head on a rock-like male shoulder that she wouldn't have traded just then for the finest down pillow in Scandinavia. "I'd hoped Birger would show up, but I never dreamed you'd be with him."

"Believe me, Birger deserves all the credit." Ross's voice was muffled as he rested his chin against the top of her head. "He was keeping an eye on Raoul and saw him get into a cab to follow you when you left the hotel. He followed both of you in his own car and saw Raoul go aboard the canal boat at the last minute after you'd gotten settled at the bow. Birger knew you'd be safe enough during the tour, so he drove back to the hotel to find me."

"I thought you'd gone to the embassy."

"I had, my love. But after I'd taken care of the formalities for our getting married, I ran across a lawyer friend of mine in the trade section. He knew about my business connections and mentioned that Raoul recently was involved in some very questionable dealings here in Scandinavia."

Ross went on in a wry tone, "After I told him that I had carried Raoul's luggage across the border today, I was firmly requested to go back to the hotel and turn the stuff over to the Danish authorities."

"That's when you ran into Birger at the hotel?"

He nodded. "After he brought me up-to-date, it only took a minute with the porter to find that you'd taken Raoul's attaché case with you."

"Just because I didn't want it to get mislaid. Of all the idiots . . ."

"You can make that two idiots," Ross said grimly. "I was the one who brought it from Helsinki in the first place." He took a deep breath. "Anyhow, we set out after you with the Danish security guard that the embassy had corralled to take custody of Raoul's luggage."

"He was the man in the uniform a few minutes ago?"

"Yes, and I'm damned glad he came along. He was the only one of us who knew about the rest stop at the end of the canal tour. We split up to look for you when we got to that neighborhood. Fortunately the guide eventually remembered your going over the bridge."

"It was a glimpse of Birger . . . I was terrified that he was waiting for me."

"So he surmised. He ran back to collect us, but by that time, Raoul was closer on your heels than we were, and we almost lost your trail. The secu-

rity guard finally discovered a news vendor who
had seen a pint-sized tourist heading for this
church. The rest, you remember."

"Parts of it I'd just as soon forget." She felt his
arm tighten protectively, and took a deep breath.
"But first . . . tell me who Birger really is."

"What you mean is . . . who pays his salary?"
Ross moved his chin softly against her hair.
"Damned if I know. All he volunteered was that
Raoul had some Finnish harbor and airport speci-
fications that were classified material. They were
to be delivered to a buyer here in Copenhagen.
Birger learned that much from Margareta. Apparently she was given this chance to make amends for
some of her mistakes in the past."

"But who was buying?" Lynda wanted to know.

"Birger wasn't talking on that either. And I'm
damned sure that the Danish authorities aren't
going to be a fund of information."

"Maybe your friend at the embassy . . ."

"My friend at the embassy will inform me that
we're well out of it and suggest that we concentrate on the Riviera for a honeymoon. Speaking of
that . . . it's getting late. We'd better be going."

Lynda squinted as she checked the face of her
watch. Then she frowned at the dial and held it to
her ear. As Ross started to stand up, she said, "We'll
have to tell the man who plays the carillon that his
clock is wrong. He was twenty minutes off—the
guidebook says the concerts are supposed to be on
the hour."

"You underestimated your rescue forces," Ross

said, assisting her to her feet. "We had to find something to cover the noise we made coming up the stairs after you. Raoul might have panicked, and we couldn't take a chance on that. The bells sounded like the best idea. We hustled the old gentleman by the cash box into service. Thank God it worked." Ross didn't give her time to wonder what would have happened otherwise. "Now, my dear Miss Garrett . . . do you think we could finally set about getting married?"

Her lips parted in surprise. "You mean today?"

A grin flickered over his face. "Certainly I mean today. Nothing's impossible if two people put their minds to it. Besides"—his tone was solemn—"after what I've been through, I'd be afraid to sleep alone."

From then on, everything went smoothly. With official approval from the embassy, it was simple to obtain the consent of the Anglican priest at the English church. The wedding ceremony was held at seven that evening, and an impromptu reception took place in the rector's home afterward.

A little later, the newlyweds found time to stroll along the splendid Langelinie promenade to see the Little Mermaid statue in the yacht harbor.

"Because," as Lynda told Ross, "today's the day for happy endings, and that was another fairy tale that came true."

When they had dinner and completed some long-distance phone calls from their comfortable hotel room overlooking Tivoli Gardens, it was very late indeed.

Ross discovered his bride sipping champagne and watching the closing fireworks display from the Danish amusement park when he emerged from taking a shower. He tightened the belt on his robe as he moved across to Lynda's quiet figure by the bedroom window. "Caught in the act!" He dropped a quick kiss at the soft curve of her neck as he reached for the champagne bottle resting in a bucket of ice by her side. "Good thing there's some left. I didn't know you were a solitary closet drinker."

"This is the bedroom . . . not the closet. A different thing entirely," she informed him austerely. "You've missed most of the fireworks."

"Oh, I wouldn't say that."

Her complexion took on color at his drawled comment. "Idiot! You know what I mean."

"Uh-huh." He brushed his lips across her flushed cheekbone. "I do indeed."

"Darling . . . let me put down this champagne," she protested breathlessly a minute later. "I don't want to spill it." It was later still when she burrowed her head into the lapels of his robe and said, "I can't believe this is real. That we're here together, and so . . ."

"Legally and thoroughly married." He pretended to grumble. "You *would* insist on the technicalities. Now, a Scandinavian woman would have taken a different attitude."

Her shoulders shook with laughter. "It's a good

thing I saved you from further temptation. Think what a well-ordered life you'll lead from now on."

"No wonder they call women the deadliest of the species." His grin flashed. "I wouldn't be in this fix if you hadn't enticed me in the first place."

She pushed back to protest. "I did no such thing!"

"Don't argue with your lord and master," he said, clamping her head back against his chest. "What chance did I have with you draped in robes and towels all over Finland and Russia? Naturally, it made me curious. . . ."

"Naturally."

"Well, if you looked that good *in* a towel," he argued defensively, "I wondered how you'd look without one. Like a little while ago—it was a great improvement." He could feel her bury her nose more determinedly in his chest as she refused to look up. "Think of the money we can save on the laundry from now on."

"I'll remember." Her head did come up then in response to his teasing, but the love reflected in her delicate features made Ross sober instantly, and he tightened his arms about her.

"There's so much more to it than that, dearest heart," he said. "I wish I could tell you properly." His look suddenly became mocking, more like the tall stranger Lynda had known in the beginning. A man who had walked in her life and, after a few days, had become her whole existence. "I guess Shakespeare said it best," Ross went on awkwardly.

"That shows how far gone I am, for God's sake— quoting poetry at midnight!"

She reached up to feather a soft kiss on his chin. "I think," she replied gently, "that quoting poetry on a honeymoon doesn't mar a man's reputation forever. According to the almanac, it's still permissible if the moon is full."

"I'm glad." His eyes glinted at her teasingly, but the timbre of his voice was rough and deep. "At least I'm in season. Well, my love, listen and remember. There's a sentence in *A Midsummer Night's Dream* that says, 'For you, in my respect, are all the world.' That's what you meant to me two minutes after we met on that street in Helsinki. What you'll be for the rest of our lives together."

"Oh, darling . . ." Lynda's words were the barest whisper as her arms went up around his neck.

"But we've talked enough." Ross's hands moved over her with sure possession, and he bent to kiss the silken hollow between her breasts. "Right now, we have other things to do."

About the Author

Glenna Finley is a native of Washington State. She earned her degree from Stanford University in Russian Studies and in Speech and Dramatic Arts, with emphasis on radio.

After a stint in radio and publicity work in Seattle, she went to New York City to work for NBC as a producer in its international division. In addition, she worked with the "March of Time" and *Life* magazine.

As a producer, she had her own show about activities in Manhattan, a show that was broadcast to England. The programs were similar to those of the "Voice of America."

Though her life in New York was exciting, she eventually returned to the Northwest where she married. Currently residing in Seattle with her husband, Donald Witte, and their son, she loves to travel, and draws heavily on her travels and experiences for the novels that have been published. Her books for NAL have sold several million copies.